MW01489129

FROM G TO PG TO R TO X

stephen c. bird

Copyright © 2022 Stephen C. Bird

All rights reserved.

Cover Design by Stephen C. Bird.

Copyright © 2022

Illustrations by Stephen C. Bird

Copyright © 2019, 2020, 2021, 2022

Hysterical Dementia

Print ISBN: 979-8-218-02391-1

eBook ISBN: 979-8-218-02392-8

DEDICATED TO

Anne L. Bird (1927-2020)
Charles A. Bird (1915-2005)

TABLE OF CONTENTS

THE WALK-IN CLOSET THAT LEADS TO THE ATTIC

The two of them were walking through a tunnel that ended who knows where. The corridor was lit by wall lamps fit with amber-colored bulbs -- Long stretches of pitch black separated the lamps from one another. While they moved through the dark intervals between the lamps -- The two of them couldn't see their hands in front of their faces. They moved on blindly, on faith, not knowing what lay ahead … The width of the underground passage seemed to fluctuate. At times, the wall lamps appeared to be within arm's reach – At other times, they shimmered in the distance like reflections dancing on water … The two of them were being pushed along by a gentle, whistling wind -- They walked on slowly, in shock … Submerged in a dream. They'd lost all sense of time – How long had she been gone? A day, a month – A year? And how long had they been walking down this path?

Since losing their mother (hereafter "Mother") all of their illusions, from every stage of their lives -- Had been shattered. Since Mother had left them -- It was as if the entire history of each of their lives had been washed out to sea … For the two of them, it was a time of questioning – "Who was she? Did we even know her? What did it all mean? Why did the Universe choose this woman to be our mother?"… In high school, if one of their classmates had written: "What is the meaning of life?" in their respective yearbooks – They would have taken that as a joke. And even now, maybe they were wasting their time -- Giving "meaning" a second thought. Perhaps meaning was just a concept -- Maybe everything that happened in the Universe was merely random … The two of them knew that they'd have to start all over, as they'd done in their late teenage years, when they'd first faced the prospect of their upcoming adulthoods. Only this time around, they were much more vulnerable – As Mother wasn't there to guide them. They'd been cast adrift and were now treading water, as if they were two eleven-year-old boys once again … How would they carry on? The foundation that had kept them rooted in, and anchored to, their lives -- Had crumbled. It was as if they'd arrived at an impasse on a mountain road where boulders from an avalanche blocked the way … And all that they could manage to do, was to stand there and stare at the majesty of those massive rocks, as the dust slowly settled ... How could they go on? They felt like they were watching an enormous iceberg, calved from an ice sheet that was floating out to sea -- To gradually melt, dissolve and become one with the ocean ... Mother's disappearance had made everything final, definitive, irreversible – Written in stone. And even though their father (hereafter "Father") had died fourteen years earlier – They were reexperiencing his absence as well, as if closure had never been achieved after his death. It was as if they were also mourning him -- For the first time ... But the loss of Father would never compare to that of Mother -- The void left by Mother's death was elemental ...

Mother's two sons, Sunnie and his brother (hereafter "Brother") -- Felt the loss within their bones. They'd taken shape inside of Mother; they'd developed within Mother -- They'd lived inside of Mother as they'd metamorphosed into recognizably human forms. They'd spent the dawn of their lives materializing within her ... And yet -- "Who was Mother?" The answer to that question was a mystery beyond their comprehension ... This place, this tunnel (that the intrusive, unwelcome presence of mortality had led both of them to) was an underworld, a subterranean alternate reality ... They kept moving, undaunted by the pitch-black darkness that was intermittently illuminated by wall lamps with amber lights. Strangely, they found their journey to be soothing – They took comfort in the sound of the whistling wind … They continued on, in limbo, in a haze -- Not rushing … They were advancing, going at a pace -- This was what they had to do and time had to be taken to do it … It was a process -- They didn't know how long it would last; they hadn't yet realized that they'd never be finished …

Mother was gone, but Sunnie and Brother still couldn't believe it – That reality was too harsh to accept. They were crushed, devastated, trauma-tized – Blindsided … While he was growing up -- Brother had not always wanted to be bothered with Sunnie, though the two of them shared many inter-ests. One thing they absolutely had in common was this: Enthusiastic participation in the trashing of both Mother and Father – While they'd been alive … But now, all was forgiven; they were seeing their parents, who they'd taken for granted and who'd often been the bane of their respective existences – In a new light. However -- None of this was shared between the two of them openly. They weren't bonding over Mother's having transitioned to the Great Beyond, because each of them viewed her differently – They saw her from different angles. They each knew their own, unique version of Mother -- They weren't even mourning the same person … In a perfect world – This loss would have brought them together. Instead

-- The two of them remained isolated within their own individual experience of grief ... Sunnie and Brother were now walking down a pathway revealed to them by a once-in-a lifetime milestone – With a very limited understanding of what one another was going through. Soon enough, the two of them would go back to their separate worlds, to the places where they lived and worked – And to their own, private experiences of what Mother had meant to them and how they'd have to let her go. Maybe they'd even have to deny the fact of her death, for the sake of their own survival … Perhaps they'd just choose to not deal with it at all; they'd block it out – If the loss ended up being too unbearable to face …

On the first of February – Sunnie moved into a fifth-floor apartment of a building that had been constructed in 1930. The apartment building stood on one of the tree-lined main venues of Small City -- Where he'd grown up. Small City was located in the western zone of the Blue-Purple Sub-Region, Northeastern Region, Amourrica Profunda, God-Wanna, Blue Green Planet … Sunnie now lived nearby Mother – He'd moved back to the area to spend time with her during her decline. He began to visit Mother frequently; but the visits were always painful, since it was obvious from Mother's progressively deteriorating condition -- That she wouldn't last long … After his first three weeks in the apartment

– Sunnie started to settle in. He was finally enjoying some time off – There was no work to do, no errands to run, no business to be taken care of … In his flat, the translucent, beige-colored shades were always closed -- They'd come with the apartment, but Sunnie saw no need to buy newer and better blinds. And so even during the daytime -- The interior of the apartment remained in permanent twilight … From the center of the south-facing wall of the apartment's living room -- One passed through a rounded archway and into a miniscule hallway. From this hallway, one had access to three rooms and a closet: To the left was the bathroom; diagonally to the left was the first bedroom; diagonally to the right was the second bedroom – And directly to the right was the hallway closet (a small walk-in closet). Behind the back wall of the hallway closet – Was an even smaller, compact closet that was part of the second bedroom. The entrance to the second bedroom was directly across from the bathroom door. The first bedroom shared a wall with the bathroom -- As well as a common wall with the second bedroom. The second bedroom was used as storage space …

As Sunnie passed by the open door of the second bedroom (which he also referred to as *the attic*) … He thought he saw something out of the corner of his eye. It was a flicker, a glimmer of light -- That seemed to have bounced off of the full-length mirror that was attached to the outside of the attic's closet door ... *Where had this light come from?* Even when the living room was fully illuminated, its light did not reach into either the bathroom, the bedroom or the attic. Normally if Sunnie was at home at dusk -- The lights in the bathroom, bedroom and attic were turned off. Once full-on evening arrived -- Those rooms were dark ... Sunnie was sure that he'd seen something -- Something was in the attic ... He turned off all of the lights in the apartment – And attempted to quell his fear as he returned to the attic entrance. Against his better judgment – He stared into the darkness of the attic ... The area in front of the southern wall of the attic was dimly lit – As light from the streetlights outside filtered in through the shade covering the lone window, in the center of the southern wall ... He felt a chill and then the goosebumps came ... A shadowy figure – Stood in front of the closed, beige-colored window blind ... What Sunnie was observing was a warped, vaguely monstrous, subhumanoid form. He turned on the harsh overhead light in the miniscule hallway to get a better look -- With the appearance of that light, the figure remained ... The specter was lean -- But not muscular; it was five feet, seven inches tall. It had two unusual ears, that looked like horns; the ear-horns slanted upwards at a very slight angle – They were practically horizontal. The face and features of the figure were so vague as to be indistinct – The head looked like an upside-down triangle with blunted corners. Its arms were long and skinny -- With long, thin fingers ending in what appeared to be sharp nails. The phantom didn't look feminine, but not particularly masculine either – It was androgynous, or even neutral. The legs, like the arms -- Were also long and skinny. The feet had long thin toes and sharp nails ... The shadowy creature began to fade away gradually; fifteen seconds later -- It was gone ...

For the next five weeks, whenever Sunnie peered into the evening gloom of the attic while passing by – The wraith was there, in either one of three positions: (1) in front of the window shade; (2) in the southwest corner, next to the window, facing the doorway of the attic closet; or (3) directly in front of Sunnie (as he looked straight ahead, from *the attic* entranceway) in the northwest corner of the room, next to the attic closet ... The specter's presence was benign – It made no aggressive, threatening moves ... Then one night, when Sunnie looked into the attic -- The eerie figure was standing in front of the lone window. It began to change, to dissolve – It turned into a dark cloud that slowly started to fill up the room; there were even tiny flashes of lightning within the cloud. The cloud kept expanding ... All of a sudden, the cloud was moving out of the attic – Filling up the miniscule hallway and then the living room with gray-black smoke. Sunnie's eyes began to water – Shortly thereafter, he was coughing and waving away the smoke … Then he lost consciousness …

He awoke to find himself lying on his back – In front of the hallway. The smoke had dissipated – The air was now clear. He stood up, entered the vestibule -- And walked into the attic. He turned on the light – A comfortless, circular overhead light that was connected to an ugly ceiling fan. Everything in the attic remained as it had been – Before the exodus of the specter, in the form of a gray-black cloud. Sunnie turned off the light and then went back into the living room – He sat down in front of his desktop computer to go through his emails …

Then one day, in the late afternoon, two months after he'd moved in, Sunnie received a call from the head nurse -- Who worked at the senior retirement complex where Mother lived. She informed him that Mother had died … He was in shock; his thoughts were a blur – A sea of memories began to wash over and through him … He remembered a photograph of Mother and himself from 1971 – It was a good memory and one of the few … Mother and Sunnie were in the dining room of the family's two-story colonial home in Small City – The house had been built in 1960. As he recalled, Mother was smiling at him as he was thinking of a wish, before blowing out the candles on a cake made for his eleventh birthday. He was sitting at a rectangular, mahogany dining table with rounded corners – Covered with an olive-green tablecloth. The wallpaper in the dining room was beige and was decorated with seafoam- and dark-green floral designs. The cake in the photo was a chocolate cake, with buttercream frosting and for some reason – There was only frosting on the top of the cake. Just a small portion of its side had been frosted -- The birthday cake had been neglected … Mother was wearing a cadet blue cardigan sweater, faded mauve turtleneck, dark blue slacks -- And stylish gray sneakers. Her eyes were light green -- Her dyed reddish-blonde hair was combed back, in a mid-1960s hairstyle still common among suburban women in 1971 … In another photo of this same birthday party, perhaps taken by Father -- Sunnie was clenching his teeth and smiling angrily. And he wasn't trying to be funny -- The subtext was real … Because like Mother, who'd perfected the art of smiling her way through difficult situations -- Sunnie was angry. Unlike Mother, Sunnie showed his anger in its unadulterated form -- *Why pretend? So what if he was mad at the world – Why should he have to hide that?* From that point on, he'd lead with a bitterness inspired by his dark side – His anger would eventually flower into rage. But it wasn't until after Mother's death -- That Sunnie finally realized how much that rage had damaged him … During the first year after Mother's passing -- Sunnie would regularly picture her asleep, in what may have been the afterlife. She wasn't enjoying a comfortable repose – She was tormented, just as she'd been in life. Which also made sense to Sunnie -- As he did not believe in the expression *rest in peace*. He believed that the soul would be transformed or reincarnated -- *Mother will transmigrate*, he convinced himself.

One night, Sunnie had a dream -- In which he saw Mother, in the upstairs bedroom of a three-story house built in 1910 … *The room was lit in a chiaroscuro style. Mother stood in the foreground – Where there was light. The background was a combination of sepia and dark brown that blended into black. Sunnie only saw Mother's face in profile in this vision. She was standing next to a bed – Wearing powder blue flannel pajamas. The bed was made up with clean white sheets -- With a plain white cotton bedspread on top. She was walking towards a white wooden door that was next to the head of the bed -- To exit the bedroom. But she never left the room -- She stopped before the door … Why did she hesitate? What awaited her on the other side of the bedroom door? …* What Sunnie hadn't noticed, during his waking hours – Was that Mother was indeed hovering nearby. She hadn't moved on yet -- In whatever way one moves on after death. She'd been trying to contact Sunnie – But he either hadn't been listening, couldn't hear her, or didn't want to hear her. If only he'd been open to sensing her presence – He would have known that she was there. But Sunnie was blocked; it was impossible for him to relax enough -- To be able to access his extra-sensory perception. He was agitated and preoccupied with fear – The fear of life, living, dying, death and of whatever happens after life ends ...

The generic apartment, in the senior retirement complex, in which Mother spent her final twelve years -- Was well-appointed, yet modest. The walls were painted a dull shade of white -- The décor was bourgeois, mundane. Paintings and watercolors, most of them executed in drab earth colors – Covered much of the wall space. Mother was a slob and the place looked lived-in – For all of her life, she'd either been comfortable being surrounded by chaos, or simply lacked the wherewithal to *make everything nice* ... Her flat included a master bedroom, a large bathroom with a shower and a medium-sized walk-in closet -- The adjacent living room included a small dining area. From the living room, a doorway next to a window -- Led to a screened-in, south-facing balcony with a cement floor. The balcony looked out over a black asphalt parking lot -- With powerful floodlights and painted yellow lines demarcating each parking space. Across from the southern side of the parking lot and the drainage canal that surrounded the property – Were unexceptional one- and two-story houses, set back from the road. Each of those houses was bordered on three sides -- By tall, silver-blue evergreen trees.

French doors separated the living room from a den that functioned as a combined office-TV room. The medium-sized kitchen was on the northern side of the apartment -- Adjacent to the living room's small dining area. A window-sized space had been cut through the wall -- To join the kitchen with the dining section. An archway separated the kitchen from the front hallway which included the front door – There was a wide closet (with a narrow depth) across from the archway entrance to the kitchen. A short corridor led from the front hallway to a washer-dryer combo on the left – And then straight ahead to a second, smaller bathroom with a bathtub-shower combination. To the right of the second bathroom was the guest bedroom that included a walk-in closet with floor-to-ceiling shelves on its back wall – That wall was adjacent to the second bathroom. The closet shelves were crowded with possessions that Mother refused to let go of … On its western side, the guest bedroom shared a common wall with the den. On the other side of the east-facing wall of the guest bedroom – Was the neighbors' apartment. Those neighbors watched television with the volume turned up early mornings, which always awakened Sunnie whenever he stayed in the guest bedroom -- Infuriating him to no end … On the ceiling of the guest bedroom's walk-in closet -- There was a panel. Sunnie didn't know what was above the panel or what it led to. While Mother had been alive and living in that apartment – He'd never asked about, or investigated, what was up there. *Then one night -- Sunnie had another dream.*

[As the dream begins – Sunnie's asleep in the guest bedroom. Mother's apartment is cloaked in darkness.]

In the dream … Sunnie woke up and noticed, looking northward from the bed where he was sleeping – That the door of the walk-in closet was open and its overhead light was on. This alarmed him; he stared into the lit-up closet for a minute or so – Why was the light turned on? He hesitated out of fear -- But then forced himself to get up from the bed. He went to the kitchen to fetch a flashlight and then returned to the walk-in closet. There was a cord with a bell-shaped plastic handle attached to the wooden ceiling panel – He pulled the cord down to open the panel. A folding wooden ladder was attached to the panel's backside. He prepared the ladder for his ascent and then armed with the flashlight -- He climbed up until he was halfway through the opening of the attic entrance. While still standing on the ladder -- He pointed the flashlight to his right … A single lightbulb, with a string and a tiny, bell-shaped aluminum handle on its end – Was revealed. He stepped up and into the attic, went over to the lightbulb, pulled the string to turn the light on -- And shut off the flashlight. The room was clean and dry and there was practically nothing in it. It was an ordinary looking attic -- With unadorned, red-dish-tan wooden beams. There was an empty card-board box on the floor -- Just beyond the circle of light cast by the bulb. Sunnie went over to the box, looked inside it … Then abruptly, everything went black …

He found himself in the hallway of a building – That appeared to have been constructed in 1930. The hardwood floors were tan-brown and a brick red runner covered the length of the corridor. Above him, there were three equidistantly-spaced, amber-colored ceiling lights – Illuminating the hallway. On either end of the corridor were sepia-colored shutters that were closed -- Sunnie didn't look to see what was behind those shutters … There were two sets of doors in the hallway -- Across from one another on each end of the corridor. Each set of doors was located four feet away from their respective hallway ends. All of the doors had faceted clear glass doorknobs. Sunnie tried to open three of the doors in the hallway – All of them were locked. When he attempted to open the fourth door – He had success. He walked through that door and closed it behind him … To his left, next to the door, was a brass wall lamp six feet off of the ground – Whose bulb emitted soft yellow light. The walls were painted beige and diagonally to his left, embedded in the far-left corner of the room -- Was an early twentieth century, dark brown wooden staircase. On that stairway, there were ten stairs going up to a landing -- Followed by another staircase, also with ten stairs, that turned to the left and continued upwards. He proceeded to walk up both sets of stairs. Upon reaching the next floor, he found himself in the middle of a second hallway -- That also had tan-brown hardwood floors with a brick red runner covering the length of the corridor. Once more, there were three equidistantly-spaced, amber-colored ceiling lights -- Illuminating the hall-way. And once again -- On either end of the corridor were sepia-colored shutters that were closed ... He continued his upward climb, always turning left and always encountering yet another staircase and yet another hallway -- That were clones of all of the pre-ceding staircases and hallways ...

Sunnie felt compelled to climb and so he didn't tire. Finally, after ascending many short flights of stairs -- He reached what seemed to be the top floor. The staircase ended, similarly to all of the previous stair-ways, in the middle of a hallway -- This corridor was identical to all of the preceding hallways ... Trusting his intuition, from the entrance to the hallway -- Sunnie chose to turn to the right. He made his way to the last right-side door at the end of the corridor. The knob was on the right side of the door – He reached for the knob with his left hand. He turned the knob and it opened with a slight click … Upon entering, to his left next to the door – There was once again a brass wall lamp six feet off of the ground; its bulb emitted soft yellow light. As before, the walls were painted beige and diagonally to his left, embedded in the far-left corner of the room -- Was an early twentieth century, dark brown wooden staircase. On that stairway, there were ten stairs going up to a landing -- Followed by another staircase, also with ten stairs, that turned to the left and continued upwards. He looked up at the landing at the top of the bottom stairway. But unlike the wall behind the previous landing, of the preceding dark brown wooden staircase in the far-left corner -- There was a lamp in the center of that wall, whose bulb emitted soft yellow light, six feet above the landing.

And right below that lamp – Was Mother. She was sitting on a plain wooden chair -- With her back straight and the palms of her hands on her knees. She was completely immobile and looked directly ahead. She appeared to be in a state of suspended animation and looked the age that she'd been when Sunnie was eleven – Forty-three years old. Her eyes were light green -- Her dyed reddish-blonde hair was combed back, in a mid-1960s hairstyle still common among suburban women in 1971. She was wearing a lightweight brown turtleneck sweater, brown plaid flare pants, brown leather shoes with chunky heels and a long, faux-gold necklace (neither Mother nor Father had ever splurged on fancy bling). She continued to look straight ahead. The expression on her face was vaguely optimistic ... Sunnie proceeded to the staircase and started to ascend. He'd only moved halfway up the stairs – When he bumped into an invisible barrier; he was being blocked. Some kind of forcefield was preventing him from getting any closer to Mother. He was able to stretch out his arms, to the right and to the left -- But it was impossible to move forward ... The occurrence of this phenomenon was in keeping with Mother's character – It was how she'd always been, while she'd been alive. The effect of the forcefield amounted to yet another dismissal; so much of the time -- Mother had just wanted to be left alone ... During her life -- Mother had been full of contradictions. And for that reason, Sunnie's relationship with her had often been difficult – It was fraught with mutual anxiety. Moreover, Sunnie was beset by his own incongruities – Which were different from those of Mother. There were many times when Sunnie had felt supported by her – Along with other times when he felt abandoned by her ... He looked at her once more, turned around, walked back down the staircase and then went out of the door through which he'd entered earlier.

After walking back into the hallway, he turned to his left – And proceeded to the farthest left-side doorway at the end of the corridor. The knob was on the right side of the door -- He opened that door with his left hand. The door budged slightly when he turned the knob -- But it was difficult to open; the bottom of the door was warped and scraping against the floor. Finally, after some struggle, the door, which opened inward -- Suddenly swung back and slammed against the wall to Sunnie's left. The door remained where it landed – As if it was stuck to the wall … And Sunnie was immediately horrified by what lay beyond the threshold of the open door; he was greeted by an overwhelmingly opaque -- Darkness. A chill emanated from beyond the open door and he started to shiver … The interior had an earthy smell, as if it was a *basement* that was full of dirt, decay, rusty metal, spider webs and crumbling brick. He stared into what could have been either a dungeon, a black hole or a potential trap -- It was as if he was encountering Nothingness … *Was this Nothingness? And what would happen to him if he stepped through this door? Did this room, this space -- Even have a floor?* … Sunnie was petrified yet transfixed -- He dared not venture beyond the threshold, lest he never return. He forced himself to retreat from that void; something was in there, something evil – That he could sense … Then the door suddenly slammed shut – It had been hit by a strong wind from that nefarious interior. He jumped back and then waited a few seconds after the door had closed. He checked the doorknob -- The door was now locked …

Although he was agnostic, in that moment, Sunnie knew that he had been blessed -- By whatever force for Good existed in the Universe. He'd rejected the essence of the *Room of Nothingness* and by doing so -- Had refused to traffic with Evil. Instead -- He chose to remain with Good. He'd saved himself and so as not to tempt fate any longer, he walked back to the top of the staircase -- In the middle of the hallway. He then made his way down the stairway -- Always turning right once he reached the next landing. Finally -- He reached the bottom of the staircase. He turned to the right and walked towards the door through which he'd entered earlier. He tried to open it – But it was locked. He started to shake the door; he was struggling now -- He was panicking and imagining that he'd be trapped in that austere interior forever. He stopped for a moment and took some deep breaths in an effort to calm himself … Then the wall lamp, to his right as he faced the door -- Began to dim gradually. Sunnie's panic was growing, but he kept breathing -- He knew that he had to remain calm … Soon it was so dark that he couldn't see his hands in front of him … Then the sound started; still distant, yet distinct – The sound of heels clomping on hardwood floors. Someone, or something – Was slowly making their way down the stairs. Sunnie continued to breathe, attempting to relax as he listened to the clomp of heels on the staircase … Then abruptly, the wall lamp by the door came back on and the space around him was once again illuminated. The clomping sound had stopped and he breathed a sigh of relief. He was now leaning against the door – With the left side of his face pressing against its surface. He wasn't sure how long he stayed that way, but eventually he turned his face to the right – And looked over towards the corner staircase …

And there, once again, was Mother -- This time standing on the middle step of the bottom flight of stairs, with her right hand on the bannister. In that moment – She appeared to be alive. She was dressed in her brown suburban outfit with her faux-gold necklace. She had a faint smile on her face -- And she looked at him, as if she wanted forgiveness, for every hurtful thing that she'd ever said or done to him -- While she'd been alive … Then the room started to darken again -- More quickly than the last time. And even though the surroundings had deepened to pitch black -- The area around Mother was now illuminated with a spotlight effect … Mother's face was now made up in clown white – The look on her face was sinister. Her eyes and lips were covered with black makeup – Her eye sockets resembled black hollows, as if her face was a skull. Her hands were covered with clown white as well – And her nails were shiny black. Her nails started growing and turned into claws. Then Mother's mouth opened -- Her teeth transformed into white fangs and the interior of her open mouth was pitch black. Her eyes were wide open, as she bared her fangs with a savage, ghastly smile -- She then extended her gleaming black claws towards Sunnie ... Then her expression began to change. She now looked sympathetic, as if she was saying: *Take my hand! I'm your Mother! I'll protect you!* She was beseeching him, imploring him to take her claw-hand (all of this being executed by her, as if she was a mime) ... Mother then put her arms down by her sides; the makeup and the claws disappeared -- She looked woebegone. Then she began to fade, ever so gradually, until she disintegrated and then vanished ... The wall lamp began to brighten -- Until the room was once again fully illuminated.

Sunnie was relieved – It was time to let go of all of his ambivalent memories of Mother, leave them in the past, move on and get back to the present. The experience that he'd just gone through was something that he wouldn't have wished on anyone. And he hoped that this specter, that may or may not have been Mother ... Had now disappeared forever and that he'd never have to see it, her or whatever it was ... Again ...

SUNNIE FINDS A PORTAL TO ANOTHER DIMENSION

A hole appeared in the floor – Right in front of Sunnie. It was a perfectly-shaped circle; an open chute reaching down, who knows how far -- To who knows where. Sunnie looked into it, but before he'd even had a chance to fully perceive what he was observing – He was sucked down into the chute … In a flash -- He was being wafted around by a breeze. He immediately lightened up and did some somer-saults, back flips, double and triple flips. There was space for that as somehow -- The diameter of the chute was much wider than he'd expected. The acrobatics came to him naturally -- As if he'd never known fear. Miraculously – He released his burden of terror and hoped his propensity for feeling dread would never return. Which was absurd, since the emotion that guided his life, above all others – Was, and always had been, fear. He'd been terrified of the compulsory dives he'd tried (and failed) to perform in high school gym class -- He now possessed the kind of courage that would have come in so handy back then … He didn't know where he was going and he didn't care -- He let go, he gave in. During his fall, the atmosphere around him modulated between black and sepia – It made no difference to him; he unconditionally embraced the darkness …

He landed softly on his feet, bending his knees slightly to cushion his touchdown – With his arms pointed straight ahead, to give himself balance. He was now standing on a bare wooden floor, in the center of an empty cylindrical-shaped room. Although there was no obvious source of illumination – He stood in crepuscular light. There were twelve wooden doors on the continuous wall of this circular space -- Each door was located ten feet away from the central spot where Sunnie stood. The dark brown doors were ten feet high -- With frosted glass doorknobs. He attempted to open one of the doors -- It was locked. The second door was locked as well -- There were no keys to be seen anywhere. Each door that he tried was locked and he started to panic -- Would he be stuck forever in yet another purgatory? Once he reached the twelfth door, he tried it, but it wouldn't open and he began to bang on the door with his fists -- Trying to smash it, to no avail. The door wouldn't budge -- And then he passed out …

When he woke up, he noticed that the last door that he'd tried to unlock – Was now open. A faint light shone from within the space beyond that open door -- He picked himself up and proceeded to explore. He walked down a dimly-lit hallway -- That followed a twisting path, a winding way that snaked to the right, to the left and then back again … This corridor, like the cylindrical room -- Was also lined with dark-brown, ten-foot wooden doors. But Sunnie had no interest in those doors now -- He was focused on moving forward … The hallway ended and Sunnie was now standing underneath a rounded archway -- Looking into the living room of a pre-war apartment; the place appeared to have been constructed in 1930. On the wall opposite from where he stood, were two antique copper wall lamps with glowing red lightbulbs -- And a square beveled mirror, encased within a shiny gold-painted wooden frame. The mirror was centered in-between the two wall lamps -- The top edge of the mirror aligned with the bottom edge of each light fixture. The walls were painted eggshell. The hardwood floors were tan-brown and were covered with blue, gray, black and white rectangular area rugs that featured a mix of abstract and geometric patterns. As he scrutinized the details and took everything in, in a flat that looked strangely familiar -- The living room transformed … Huge gray-black tree trunks were now embedded in the walls of the living room's southwest and southeast corners – The bark of the trees appeared to have been charred by fire. The roots of those trees spread across the floor -- The end of each individual root was tipped with what looked like the dangerously sharp claws of a gigantic raptor. Each tree grew upward, into what was presumably the upstairs apartment -- Who knows how much higher those tree trunks extended and whether they burst through the roof and out into the night sky? For it was definitely night in this space … Additional lighting was provided by a sleek, vintage porcelain lamp – A dark aqua lamp, speckled with indigo. The body of that lamp had the shape of a large glass Perrier bottle – And was topped off with a sky-blue shade. It stood on a small, square dark brown wooden table with black steel legs -- In the northeast corner of the living room … It was quiet in that room -- There wasn't a sound to be heard from outside. Sunnie felt electricity in the air – He was intrigued …

On both the eastern and the western end of the wall, featuring the two copper light fixtures with red lightbulbs and the square gold-framed mirror – Were rounded archways leading to other rooms. The eastern archway led to a small dining room next to a kitchen. The western archway led to a long hallway, on the other side of the kitchen -- Which ended at the ten-foot high, mahogany door that served as the entrance to the apartment … The west-side corridor was exceedingly long -- It went on for miles and miles. And yet somehow, it remained within the interior of the flat -- It was an optical illusion; the front door was so close and yet so far ... Standing underneath the east-side archway was a ten-foot-tall female leg – With a very big foot. She was wearing a black patent-leather pump, with a thick stout heel in an early 1930s style – And a dark purple fishnet stocking. The top of the thigh that was "her", continued up and through the ceiling, breaking through the archway in the process -- The width of the thigh corresponded to the diameters of the nearby tree trunks ... The Leg (hereafter "Momma Leg") brusquely broke the silence and began to address Sunnie in a thundering voice, with a posh accent -- She spoke in the manner of an aggressive, abusive dominatrix. Although she had no visible mouth -- The disembodied sound of Momma Leg's cruel voice reverberated throughout the room ...

Momma Leg: *Get on the floor, little boy! You dickless, thumb-sucking choir boy -- Oh, you must have been such a precious, adorable little sweetheart when you brought home your drawings that Mommy would put on the refrigerator for you! You were such a sweetie with your blossoming creativity! Such a wiwwle tweetie pie wif youw dwawings fow the wefwigewatow! But now you're all grown up, hell you're middle-aged -- And Mommy's dead. And you'll just have to fucking get over it, because you're not the only one, it happens to everyone else – What, do you think you're special? Do you fancy yourself as "terminally unique"? And you know why I'm telling you this? Because I want to treat you like shit! That's my raison d'etre! That's right, the reason why I wake up with a smile on my face every morning – Is because I know that I'm able to maintain control over multitudes of weak, worthless boy-men like yourself! Who are waiting for me to humiliate them! By the way – You're not a boy-man; you're not a boy-woman either! You're not even a girly-man – Or a girly-boy!! You know what you are? You're a girly-girl! And when you were a child – The men who fancied themselves to be manly shamed you for being a girly-girl! And that's what I'm doing to you now -- Even though you never consented to be treated this way! I DON'T NEED YOUR CONSENT! I DON'T CARE ABOUT YOUR CONSENT! YOU DO WHAT I SAY – MY WAY OR THE HIGHWAY! Yes, this qualifies as abuse and as much as you may protest that you don't like it – There are so many others who complain, as you do, and then they return for repeat sessions! Accept your destiny, accept your fate – You are a girly-girl and you're never going to change! Yes, this is a free consultation -- But I'm certain that you'll come back for more sessions and pay me what I deserve! You'll pay me whatever I want – You know why? Because I'm a PREDATORY CAPITALIST and you are my PREY. EAT! PREY! LOVE! That's my motto – Well, almost! I'll prey on you and eat you – But there's no* way that I'm ever going to love you! "What's Love Got To Do With It?" … If you want to delude yourself by calling this love – Go ahead, I don't care how you qualify our relationship! Just make sure that you keep those thoughts to yourself – I do the talking around here and you will only speak to me when I command you to do so! I didn't choose you – You chose me! You will become my customer and the sole purpose of our transactions will be for me to debase and degrade you -- As much as that's humanly possible! Are you my P@¥p@L? Are you going to pay me with P@¥p@L? You'd better fucking pay up -- P@¥p@L! … Now it's time for me to set up some ground rules and explain how you'll have to behave for Momma Leg … First of all: Get down on your knees and lick the sole of my shoe! And then clean the surrounding floor with your tongue as well! Feel the dirt on your tongue – Relish it! And leave your clothes on – I don't want to be disgusted by your flabby body and your teeny tiny wee wee … Teeny Tiny Wee Wee … TEENY TINY WEE WEE! You know, I may just jam my heel up your ass tonight! I sincerely hope your asshole is clean -- Did you douche? Are you fully lubricated? I hope you're prepared! Do you like pain? You're not afraid of a little pain – Are you? Isn't that what you want? But then again -- Who cares what you want?! Only I know what you want and I will tell you what you want! You've done nothing in your life to deserve anything but pain, suffering and humiliation – And I'm so glad *that's how it's worked out for you, because torturing you gives me such pleasure! It gives me such pleasure to give you what you deserve! You're a worm -- You fucking worm ... Worm ... WORM!! There's nowhere to run – Nowhere to hide! PEEK-A-BOO! Keep licking the floor! The dirt is a divinely delicious delicacy – And you know it! And don't forget to lick the top and sides of Momma's shoe, as well – Until it gleams with a lustrous brilliance!*

Sunnie continued to obey Momma Leg without question ... He was tied to Momma Leg's apron strings, in the same way he'd always been attached to his deceased Mother ... He'd never defy Momma Leg -- Which was something that he'd never admit to anyone. He was a masochist submissive who felt compelled to accept the severity of Momma Leg's sadism. He didn't like the way she treated him – He just had to take it, as the only thing of which he was worthy was punishment. He was conflicted; he was okay with being trapped – And yet he wanted to escape. For that reason -- He wished he was a cat that could scurry away to obscure itself underneath a car and continue to observe unseen. Whenever Sunnie found himself in the *fight or flight syndrome* – He became the metaphorical cat that could sprint up to the top of a tree in seconds flat. And once he reached the upper branches, no-one could get to him and he could finally relax – And watch the world pass by below, from a safe distance …

Momma Leg: *One last thing: I just wanted to let you know that whichever color you represent on the Reign-Beau of the LGBTQIA spectrum -- I'm not interested! Whatever you are – Be it lesbian, gay, bisexual, trans male, trans-female, queer, intersex or asexual – I don't care! And whatever you do sexually, and whoever you do it with, is of no concern to me because – I'm entirely focused on abuse and that's all I have to offer you, or anyone else, for that matter! I don't want anything from you, besides your money, your blind devotion – And your awareness that you disgust me and that you are a W0RM! Be gone from my sight and I can't wait for you to come crawling back to me! IS THAT 1000% CLEAR? NOW GET THE FUCK OUT OF HERE!*

While speaking her final words, Momma Leg disintegrates and then disappears. The two corner trees with their ravaged black bark and roots vanish as well.

Two women appear. They are caustic -- Yet friendly. Harsh, loud and wild – And full of humor. And unlike Momma Leg. they're fun to be around -- Until you become the target of one of their jokes and have to defend yourself against their slings and arrows … These two females are sitting in the northeast and southeast corners of the living room. Each of them has sunk down into the plush comfort of two identical rosewood Deco armchairs – Upholstered in pine green velvet … Sunnie watches the two of them from the southwest corner of the living room. They are oblivious to his presence …

PAMM AND REMMY
APPEAR FROM OUT OF NOWHERE

Pamm Demmyck: (addressing an imaginary audience) Hi – How are you? I'm Pamm – Pamm Demmyck!

Remmy Dessyvyr: (also addressing an imaginary audience) And I'm Remmy -- Remmy Dessyvyr. Unlike Pamm -- I don't waste my time with salutations! So don't tell me how you are – Because I don't care!

Pamm: (gives Remmy a hostile look, then looks around suspiciously) Where's Momma Leg? I hope she's gone forever! Her attitude and moods are such a downer!

Remmy: Yeah …. Why so serious – Momma Leg?! By the way – What kind of name is Momma Leg?! Life's too short, she's a drag -- A complete nightmare! Don't come around here no more -- Momma Leg!

Pamm and Remmy both get up and step away from their rosewood Deco armchairs and stretch out their arms to each other using formal balletic gestures – As if they're about to curtsey one another in the style of an eighteenth-century Baroque dance … In that moment, they imagine themselves to be present *within a Rococo scenario, replete with suitable props (for both the gentlemen and the ladies): white powdered wigs; elaborately embroidered gold and silver waistcoats, breeches and gowns; and gold and silver shoes, with ornate bejeweled buckles and stout heels … Everything shimmers in a half-light provided by candelabras – Harpsichord music is heard in the background … Pamm and Remmy make awkward attempts at gracing one another with delicate gestures. But they quickly abandon those efforts to then face each other, take one another's hands and hold them below each other's chins – While hesitantly starting to sing "Don't Come Around Here No More" softly to one another … They stare into one another's eyes with sincere gazes -- In a show of faux intimacy. They then break off their singing -- And begin to laugh raucously and scream in delight …*

Remmy: (*crying*) I miss our drunken karaoke nights! Those were the days!

Pamm gives Remmy a micro-moment of empathy. Then she puts on her angry face.

Pamm: (*giving Remmy the evil eye, while addressing an imaginary audience*) You best get outta town by sundown -- Momma Leg!

Remmy: That's right grrrrrrrl – Get the HAYLLLL out of this one-horse town and find yourself a new rodeo! Or thay'll most assuredly be a shootout at that salacious saloon you been sallying around at!

Then Eight Octopus Tentacles (the head of the octopus remains out of view) in various shades of pink – Appear in the rounded archway through which Sunnie entered the living room earlier. Each tentacle is covered with suckers on its underside.

Eight Octopus Tentacles: (*addressing an imaginary audience*) Greetings – I'm Hydra – Hydra Whorror Kween! (*pauses*) I'm very nice, sweet, gentle, considerate -- And I'd never hurt a soul! At least, that's what I tell people – Who'll discover the malevolence of my dark and destructive moods soon enough! Furthermore -- If I happen to veer over into my not-so-nice frame of mind -- It's going to get very, very bad between us! Whether it's fair or not! Life isn't fair! And so why do I have to be? WATCH OUT! I'M MANIC! DO YOU WANT TO EXPERIENCE MY MANIA? ... And when my out-of-control glee gets the best of me, other sabotaging emotions take over and crowd out my joy – Don't tell me that you haven't been warned! Because when the ship goes down – I like to take at least one person with me! (*with faux sweetness*) I may just attack you, unexpectedly, with my tentacles – And things could get rough! Please know that I have nothing to lose, because if I lose one of my limbs – I can grow it back! That's right -- I'm immortal! As long as I still have my head; even if I lose all of my limbs, except for one -- I can grow all the rest of my tentacles back! And I will live again! I will live forever! I can reincarnate while I'm still alive! Let's hear it for reincarnation … Reincarnation … REINCARNATION!

Abruptly, the legs of female dancers appear -- A throng of calves, thighs and feet start to kick and break through the western and southern living room walls. Each leg is adorned in sparkly gold tights; each foot is in a glittery gold shoe -- With straps and stout heels. While they kick up a storm -- Dust from the dismantled sheetrock starts to cloud up the room … Music from Lloyd Bacon's "42nd Street" starts playing … Pamm and Remmy begin laughing and screaming with delight again … Hydra Whorror Kween, in a manic mood as promised, attacks both Pamm and Remmy, but they react quickly -- Beating Hydra Whorror Kween to death with a nearby vacuum cleaner, destroying the head and all of the limbs thoroughly.

Pamm and Remmy: (*in unison*) Hydra Whorror Kween was a false friend – A *faux ami*! And that's why she deserved to die! No-one crosses Pamm and Remmy!

The gold legs and shoes begin to kick even faster … Pamm and Remmy are now doing bong hits under a blacklight in a 1973 teenage bedroom with heavy metal posters lining the walls … Music from

Lloyd Bacon's "42nd Street" morphs into glitter and glam rock with heavily amplified electric guitars and an abundance of reverb ... Every element of the current scenario begins to warp, mutate and elongate. All of the components of the present environment swirl together within a splatter painting comprised of fluorescent yellow, phosphorescent pink, dayglo green and neon orange ... Light, sound and substance blend into a mélange somewhere between the tangible and the incandescent. All of this mutating even further into an explosion of synesthesia- and chromesthesia-based chaos ... In a neighboring universe, beams of light emanating from a quasar stretch out into infinity. The activity of the quasar melds with the present setting to create a state-of-the-art interpretation of the light show at the end of "2001: A Space Odyssey" ... The omnium gatherum then expands into an inconceivably huge mass, which then rapidly contracts, as everything is pulled into a black hole, to either be extinguished forever -- Or reanimated to reappear in a parallel universe, or in whatever exists beyond that which is known.

"Turn On, Tune In, Drop Out"
Timothy Leary, 1966

PAMM AND REMMY
TRY TO WORK TOGETHER

Pamm Demmyck and Remmy Dessyvyr are once again lounging in the plush comfort of the two identical rosewood Deco armchairs upholstered in pine green velvet -- In the northeast and southeast corners of the1930 pre-war apartment living room. Sunnie is watching the two of them from the southwest corner of the same room. Pamm and Remmy are unaware of his presence – Pamm's dozing off and Remmy's fast asleep.

Pamm Demmyck: (*she stirs herself from sleep and then tries to wake up Remmy*) Remmy? REMMY? Rise and shine! Time for us to continue making something of ourselves – So that someday soon we'll be lauded for our monumental contributions to the entertainment industry!

Remmy Dessyvyr: (*sluggish*) Pamm? Where am I? What's up? Are we still friends? (*reviving*) I can't believe that we're still friends!

Pamm: (*ignoring Remmy's remark*) What a great party, huh? Wow – You really tied one on!

Remmy: What party? What happened? I don't even remember being there …

Pamm: (*sharply*) THERE WASN'T ANY PARTY – OKAY?! Time to get back to work! (*reasonable*) I have some ideas for those jokes we were brainstorming about the other day. Did you forget that we're writing partners now?

Remmy: (*sarcastically*) How could I forget – With you trying to light a fire under my ass twenty-four seven!

Pamm: PLEASE STOP! (*pause*) Let's save the sarcasm for our adoring audiences, okay? Don't take them for granted, you know who I'm talking about -- Those crowds of drunken, casino-vacationing, jackpot-wishing, roulette-wheel-spinning animals and proto-fascist mobs whose laughter we depend upon -- To pay our rent?

Remmy: (*with faux excitement*) Oh my Goddess -- I love those people! Ever since I was a little girl – I dreamed of writing jokes targeted towards the delusional, barbarian hordes of which you speaketh! THE ENEMY HATH PROPAGATED ITSELF – PAMM! … But seriously -- I'm so psyched! Don't underestimate me -- I'm so down for this!

Pamm: (*businesslike*) Let's go through the list of setups. Here we go: Two ugly bitches who can't get laid walk into a bar …

Remmy: (*reactively*) Hey! Speak for yourself! What do you think you're doing? I mean, It's 2022 – Not 1972?!? Maybe you should think twice about including me in your toxic, dysfunctional stew of low self-esteem, self-hatred, sexual self-hatred, self-sabotage and misogyny! (*folding her arms and smiling icily*) The way that we'll win Pamm, in whichever perilous *boite* we happen to find ourselves – Will be to channel our inner Auntie Mames! She'll never go out of style – She'll always be a classic!

Pamm: (*steely*) Just as long as you remember one thing, Remmy – And that's this: WE'RE WRITING JOKES! NOTHING IS SACRED. Furthermore -- Those two ugly bitches are not us! Here's who they are: They're jealous, vindictive, self-hating, self-sabotaging and low self-esteem women – Who only slightly resemble us …

Remmy: (*sarcastic*) Okay – I get it! I was worried there for a minute. But now I'm completely relieved – I feel reassured to the max!

Pamm: (*starting over*) Two ugly bitches who can't get laid …

Remmy: *(interrupting)* How about this? Jane Russell, Jayne Mansfield, Hanoi Jane, Sweet Jane and *Janie's Got A Gun* walk into a bar …

Pamm: I don't like that idea, Remmy! It's such a *try-too-hard* kind of idea!

Remmy: But a setup like *two ugly bitches who can't get laid walk into a bar* is just not going to work in the context of 2022 Woke *Feminism* …

Pamm: *(adamant)* It will work! IT WILL WORK! And just because I'm not politically correct – Doesn't make me one uh them thar *deplurabibbles*! … It's not that we're so great -- In fact, we're mediocre. Neither one of us will ever get close to creating a Sistine Chapel, a Taj Mahal, a Timbuktu, the Moai Statues of Easter Island or Wagner's *Der Ring des Nibelungen* … But there's a great deal that we can accomplish with persistence alone -- And we will succeed! Confidence is everything and you've never had any (although you've managed to fake it pretty well). So thank Goddess for me! You wouldn't have the luxury and the privilege of being able to fall asleep in a rosewood Deco armchair if it hadn't been for me …

Remmy: *(yelling in a disturbingly exuberant way)* FOLLOW YOUR BLISS! LISTEN TO YOUR INNER CHILD! LISTEN TO YOUR INNER VOICE! FAKE IT TILL YOU MAKE IT! BE A NON-PERMANENT ENTITY IN THAT EPHEMERAL MOMENT THAT IS THE PRESENT! NOTHING

IS INDESTRUCTIBLE! NOTHING LASTS! (*firmly, after a pause*) … You're just pissed because I have the nerve to call you on your shit! In this instance – You are the status quo and I'm challenging that status quo! We CAN and WILL incorporate a respect for Wokeness – Into this, our current endeavor!

Pamm: (*quietly*) Are you kidding?

Remmy: (*soberly*) I know -- I'm such a hypocrite. I mean … Yes, I'm woke -- But only in a narcoleptic way.

There's a shift in Remmy's attitude – She's now staring off into space.

Remmy: (*despondent*) Pamm?

Pamm: (*with dread*) What … Remmy?

Remmy: You know I've been going through a hard time -- Right?

Pamm: (*pauses*) I wasn't sure … I didn't know if I should say anything …

Remmy: (*far away*) I miss Mommy …

Pamm: (*concealing impatience*) Of course. But we all have to go through that, at some point or another. Everybody leaves us -- Everyone dies …

Remmy: (*frantic*) Where's Mommy, Pamm? Where's Mommy? (*hysterical*) WHERE'S FUCKING MOMMY?! WHERE'S FUCKING MOMMY?! (*she extends her arms* out in front of her, with her eyes wide open, as if she were pretending to be blind) … Mommy … Mommy! … MOMMY … MOMMY! (in a baby voice) – Mommy Go Die Die! MOMMY GO DIE DIE! (sobbing) When will Mommy come back?! WHEN WILL MOMMY COME BACK?! (she starts sucking her left thumb, with her right hand clutching her left elbow) …

Pamm: (attempting compassion) I don't know where Mommy went, Remmy -- I wish I did. Maybe Mommy is no more -- Maybe there is no more Mommy … Who's to say that the soul or consciousness -- Exists after death? (pausing) Did you ever try to imagine Nothingness?

Remmy: (puts her hands over her ears) Don't you try it! DON'T YOU TRY IT! … Don't even think about it – DON'T EVEN THINK ABOUT IT! … Don't waste your time; I can't – I CAN'T!

Pamm: (vigorously shakes Remmy by the shoulders) Snap out of it – Remmy! You know how it is when people die – Your friends come out with the platitudes, such as: Mommy's in heaven now with Daddy! Mommy's seeing her friends on The Other Side! Mommy's talking to God! Or – This one: You'll always have your mother! She'll always be with you! Keep a framed portrait of your mother, illuminated by a single candle – On a small table in a corner of a dark room! Leave the room empty -- Except for the table on which the framed portrait and the candle will stand!

And don't forget this: There should never be any cur-
tains, or any other kind of covering, obscuring the win-
dows of that room at any time – Because the spirits
from the afterworld, especially those who are close
to Mommy, must not be blocked from entering! They
need to come and go as they please! Never underes-
timate the importance of this special shrine where you
can always honor Mommy! (firmly) All of that being
said, the issue still begs the question: DOES ANYONE
ACTUALLY KNOW WHERE MOMMY WENT -- REMMY?!

Remmy: (*standing up and pointing her right index*
finger at Pamm) I curse you with the power of one
thousand dying suns! (*screaming*) EVEN IF NO-ONE'S
EVER GOING TO BE ABLE TO TELL ME WHERE MOMMY
WENT -- THAT DOESN'T MAKE IT ANY LESS RELEVANT!
(*like a woman careening towards madness*) I
know what I need … Some kind of intermediary
… Someone who communes with the dead – A
medium! Yes -- That's what I require … Because in
spite of what you may believe -- I'm not sure that
Mommy's completely gone yet. I think she may be
hovering nearby ... Or chilling out in the astral plane
that she's using as her green room – It's the waiting
room for reincarnation …

Pamm: (*loudly and sarcastically*) You'll never lose your
mother! You don't have to wonder where she is – She's
living with you right now, in your heart … She's watching over you – As we speak, like a guardian angel!

(melodramatically, while gesturing in the style of a silent screen diva) … YOU ARE LIT FROM WITHIN REMMY – BY THE LIGHT OF YOUR ETERNALLY PRESENT MOTHER!

Remmy: *(with barely suppressed anger)* Maybe … All … Of … It … Really … Is … Just … Sugarcoated verses that appear on greeting cards – STRAIGHT OUTTA HALLMARK!!!! … Why should I even bother taking this conversation to a mystical, otherworldly level – With you?! *(with building hysteria) I don't care if you don't get it – I still have to say it!* WHERE'S FUCKING MOMMY?! WHERE'S FUCKING MOMMY?! MOMMY, MOMMY, MOMMY!!!! MOMMY, MOMMY, MOMMY!!!!

Pamm waits for Remmy's outburst to end.

Pamm: *(slowly and dully)* It just takes time -- You know? The process of accepting a loss. And don't expect people who haven't been through what you're going through – To sympathize … What will we do when our time comes – Remmy? Will we be able to face it? Will we?

Remmy: *(crestfallen)* I don't know … It's just that … You don't get it – YOU DON'T GET IT! You see … The only reason I'm talking to you about this is because – You're all I've got. There's no-one else – And you know why? Because everyone else is jitterbugging with the latest algorithms on Fascibook … And as much as I wish it could -- The self-help industry will not save us from death! Although, at least -- It will help us to manage our lives and to know how we can live those lives more fully. And since I'm agnostic, I choose that billion-dollar industry over organized religion, any day of the week, to worship as my golden idol ... Why should I expect my narcissistic, so-called friends, who are stuck in their silos and echo chambers – To listen to my unending, miserable monologues anymore? I mean, no matter how down and out you are – You've just gotta get back to that place where you're singing and dancing again! You've just gotta start kicking! For Chrissake – I'm not ready for the alternative! I'LL FIND MY MOJO! I'M A FIGHTER! I'M IN IT FOR THE LONG HAUL – BABY! HEY GRIM REAPER! YOU FUCK WITH ME? I FUCK WITH YOU BACK!

Remmy continues to chant while stomping her feet on the floor.

FUCK WITH ME -- FUCK WITH YOU BACK!!!
FUCK WITH ME -- FUCK WITH YOU BACK!!!
FUCK WITH ME -- FUCK WITH YOU BACK!!!
FUCK WITH ME -- FUCK WITH YOU BACK!!!

Pamm walks over to Remmy and stands by her side. She waits for Remmy's tantrum to stop.

Pamm: It's time for our song – Remmy.

Remmy: Okay.

Pamm takes a pitchpipe out of her pocket and then blows the starting note. Pamm and Remmy count to three and then begin to sing loudly in unison:

WE'RE NOT GONNA TAKE IT!
NO -- WE'RE NOT GONNA TAKE IT!
WE'RE NOT GONNA TAKE IT – ANYMORE!

They stop singing abruptly.

Remmy: (*softly*) Pamm?

Pamm: Yes – Remmy?

Remmy: I have to tell you my dream.

Pamm: (*resigned*) All right.

Remmy: (*stares off into space for a moment*) My brother Jimmie was in my dream -- But I can only recall that part vaguely. The part with Mommy I remember clearly … I can't talk to Jimmie about Mommy because he refuses to reflect. He gets stuck in this place where he's on the verge of understanding me and then – Some kind of emotional forcefield comes up and he shuts down. So we can't share our grief -- I have no idea how he's mourning. He withdraws, he goes inward -- There's no reaching him! It's no use … We all experience and process loss differently … We all know a different side of our mothers … And then, we all have to go through this on our own -- Alone …

Pamm: (*sensibly*) As for the siblings: Who knows why they think what they think? Don't waste your time trying to figure that out -- Life's too short ... I have to be frank with you -- I've haven't been through what you're going through. At least, not yet. You alluded to this earlier – You intuited where I was coming from. Point being: The things I've been saying to you -- My supposed words of comfort? You were right -- I have been using expressions that I found in greeting cards. I let greeting cards speak for me, when I have to connect with friends who are in trouble -- Since my empathy-based vocabulary is limited ...

Remmy: I knew it – I KNEW IT! (*pause*) You ... Are ... A ... Monster ...

Pamm: Yes ... I am.

Remmy is silent for a moment.

Remmy: (*takes a deep breath*) I forgive you ...

Remmy *turns her face away from Pamm and starts chanting with a lost and confused look in her eyes.*

Where's Mommy? Where's Mommy?
Where's Mommy?
Mommy, Mommy, Mommy ...
Where's Mommy? Where's Mommy?
Where's Mommy?
Mommy, Mommy, Mommy ...

Remmy begins to describe her dream.

I was walking up this endless series of stairways. I'd reach a hallway at the end of one staircase -- And the new corridor I encountered would look exactly the same as those I'd seen previously. They were always hallways with three amber-colored ceiling lights -- Spaced apart from one another other at eye-pleasing intervals. The hardwood floors were tan-brown and brick red runners covered the length of the corridors. There were sepia-colored shutters, on both ends of the hallways -- That were closed. I didn't look to see what was behind those shutters. The walls were painted beige, the wooden doors were dark brown -- The doorknobs were made of faceted clear glass ... I kept trying to open various doors – Some opened immediately; some were locked; some led to other rooms that were identical to all of the rooms that I'd encountered previously ... Finally, I tried to open a door that budged slightly when I turned the knob -- It was difficult to open. The door was scraping on the floor, but then after some prolonged effort – It gave way. After it was open, the door suddenly slammed itself against the inside wall to my left – Where as far as I could tell, it was stuck and remained flush against that wall ...

I was immediately overwhelmed by the wild, new environment that I'd just encountered. It's hard for me to accurately describe what exactly existed inside this room – All that I could perceive was color ... Neon

pink, dayglo green, fluorescent orange and phosphorescent yellow … Iron Butterfly's "In-A-Gadda-
Da-Vida" was playing -- So groovy! Encountering that
space, I felt an immediate Oneness with the Universe,
like I'd been meditating for a thousand years in the
Would Between The Whirlds (a mellow chartreuse
pastoral landscape with sky blue pools and bab-
bling bubbling brooks, where everyone is stoned
and no one is paranoid) … But then all of the trippy
colors vanished and were instantly replaced by an
overwhelmingly opaque -- Darkness … At first, I was
fearful, but it only took a moment for me to build up
my angry resistance -- And then I blew my top. I was
shouting -- NO, NO, NO! THIS IS NOT WHAT I WANT! I
WILL NOT ACCEPT THIS DARKNESS! WHERE ARE MY
PRETTY COLORS? I WANT MY PRETTY COLORS BACK!
GIVE THEM TO ME NOW! … In my panic, I began to
pray to Maya Hiyuh Powuh, Goddess of Agnosticism.
I asked her the following questions … Is the Ghost of
Timothy Leary haunting his Third-Eye Mansion?!?! That's
located at the Bitchkoch Estate, Thrillbrook, Hustler
Valley, Megajorcka, Northeastern Region, Amourrica
Profunda?!?! I WANT MY TIMOTHY LEARY THRILL PILL
-- MAYA! I WANT IT NOW AND I WON'T TAKE NO FOR
ANSWER! Where's the original 1943 LSD, the kind
that originated in Albert Hofmann's lab in Basilikum,
Schweizer-Deutschland, Old-World? Where's the kind
of acid that the Merry Pranksters were taking in 1964
-- Right before they opened up the Pandora's Box of

Tripping and turned on the burgeoning Amourrica Profundan hippie population? … But I received no word of guidance from Maya, there was no sign that she'd heard me – For all I knew, she'd abandoned me to the wilderness … And then I began to have a change of heart. Because even though I would have rather stayed in the Would Between The Whirlds – I adjusted to being enveloped in darkness; I accepted its presence … And then -- A figure appeared. At first it was indistinct, difficult to discern -- It became clearer after several moments … It was a woman -- She was illuminated, as if by a spotlight and stood in marked contrast to the pitch-black darkness surrounding her … And then I recognized her: It was Mommy as she looked in 1971, when I was age eleven … As she came into focus -- I could see that she was forty-three years old and that her eyes were dark brown. Her hair was black and combed back from her forehead. She was wearing a purple-fuchsia pants suit, an aqua and yellow-green striped rayon blouse -- And lilac vinyl open-toe high heel sandals … Seeing her like that was too much for me and once again -- I just said NO … I didn't say no to deny the clarity of my vision of her. I said NO because I didn't want to recognize the harsh reality – That she was never coming back; that she'd already been transformed into stardust … That she'd vanished, disappeared and disintegrated -- Never to be seen in her human form again …

And then I woke up.

Pamm looks at Remmy in silence.

Pamm: *(sincerely)* I'm sure that Maya Hiyuh Powuh is watching over us – And will aid us as we struggle within the confines of this patriarchal, chauvinist, sexist pig profession that we've chosen to pursue! That being said: Let us embrace the present moment – And get back to the work that is our calling. *(optimistically)* ONWARD!

Remmy sits quietly for a moment and then her face lights up.

Remmy: *(serenely)* The only thing that gives me comfort now is to think about the dystopic future that all of humanity will experience. Yes, It's a frightening reality to consider -- But it's way better than obsessing about the ghosts of my past ... *(loudly, defiantly)* ONWARD! HERE'S TO THE PRESENT MOMENT! I EAGERLY ACCEPT ALL OF THE CHALLENGES THAT LIFE HAS TO OFFER!

Pamm: All right then! We've got setups and punchlines to flesh out! So let's get back to business!

AMOURRICA PROFUNDA BECOMES MOURRZICKA

Once upon a time, in the country of Amourrica Profunda, in the continent of God-Wanna – The people lived in peace, in a civil society, agreeing to disagree and respecting each other's diverse views. Then all of that started to change. Amourrica Profunda had been in decline for decades – Its culture had been coarsening; its reputation on the world stage of the Blue Green Planet had become tarnished. The population had stopped reading books – They preferred to mindlessly scroll through social media content on their Tombphones. People stopped talking to one another – Instead, they chose complete involvement with their devices. This drove them into seclusion – To a place where their Tombphone addictions took over their lives. Despite this being an unhealthy and obsessive way of life – A lot of time was saved by being able to manage their work, social and personal lives, within a context of increased isolation ...

The headquarters of the Amourrica Profundan Governmental Apex (hereafter "APGA") -- Were located in the Off-White House on 6666 Transylvania Avenue, in the City of Bruschettya, in the metro-politan area of Kapitolya, in the Central Eastern Region. The Co-Chancellors of Amourrica Profunda, Giovanni and Juliana Azul, who'd been elected by the nation's Blue Majority -- Lived together in the Off-White House, as man and wife. Politically, Amourrica Profundans were divided into two parties – The *Blue* Majority (*Democratic*) and the *Red* Minority (*Fascist*). 51 percent of the populace supported the Blue Majority; 49 percent of the population supported the Red Minority – However, the Reds were quickly gaining in popularity, literally nipping at the heels of the Blues. In theory, it was possible to be *Purple* (*Independent*) -- But when it came time to vote in an election, the Purples had only two choices: *Red* or *Blue*. The Reds believed themselves to be patriotic, religious and conservative -- The Blues tended to be liberal, secular and progressive ... A great number of citizens were unsure about whether Giovanni and Juliana Azul would be capable of governing the nation as a whole. How would they unify the coun-try -- When the Blues and the Reds were unable to agree upon anything? And how long would this Blue interlude last, before the Reds were swept back into power, to pass authoritarian laws and implement repressive policies -- That went against the wishes of even their own constituents? The Reds conspired to discover any chance they had, no matter how remote -- To sabotage the electoral process and take back power from the Blues, by legal means. Although the Blues supported progressive policies – They were not in a position to codify those policies into law. Why? Thanks to an extraordinary increase in the prevalence of corrupt legislative practices, the Reds had strongarmed their way into positions in which they were firmly in control of policy making – Even in regions where their party was in the minority. It was and it remained -- A very divided, polarized time …

In Amourrica Profunda, corporations continued to buy huge amounts of influence through the use of lobbyists -- Who worked within the byzantine halls of the Amourrica Profundan Governmental Apex (APGA). The lobbyists had become so powerful that APGA surrendered to most of their demands. The ever-widening chasm between the rich and the poor, along with the resentment caused by pervasive economic inequality -- Had created an opportunity for extremism to flourish. Case in point: the Reds were now tempting fate, by being drawn to and then following -- Despots disguised as Pied

Pipers. These wannabe-tyrants, who'd been waiting in the wings for a beneficial *Zeitgeist* that would work in their favor, now danced their way down nihilistic political roads -- With their clueless *strong man-admiring* (and in some cases, *strong-women admiring*) adherents in tow ...

Due to all of the aforementioned, Turmerico Inflammatorio (Red candidate for chancellor) had managed to become chancellor of Amourrica Profunda – In the administration prior to that of Giovanni and Juliana Azul. Turmerico had defeated his political rival, Jillarie Klyntonstyne (Blue candidate for chancellor) who'd been favored to win the race -- Even though she'd proven to be one of the most unpopular political candidates in Amourrica Profundan history ... Inflammatorio was equally unpopular, but won the election on a technicality – Thanks to outmoded laws governing electoral processes, that had been put into place by the late eighteenth century Amourrica Profundan Founders. Those laws had ended up making it easier for the unscrupulous Reds -- To work towards their goal of achieving minority rule ...

The magical thinking behind the belief that an autocrat could save the country from a supposed cultural downward spiral – Caught on with the Red minority. Turmerico promised safety, security and prosperity – He vowed to bring back the mythical *good old days* when Amourrica Profunda had been the envy of most of the nations of the Blue Green Planet. Inflammatorio offered up a tantalizing slice of *faux nostalgia* and the Reds fell for the bait – Hook, line and sinker. He'd regularly make empty promises to his base, such as: "*Prosperity For All! No Socialist Healthcare! No More Forever Wars! Shiny New Infrastructure is on the Way! I Will Stop Immigrants from Stealing your Jobs!*" … But the elephant in the room was this: Turmerico could care less about helping the people. He was only interested in achieving absolute power – Which he'd then use to benefit himself, his family and his *oprichniki*. Inflammatorio would enrich his family, by means of nepotism -- And his sycophantic, *patriot* disciples, by means of tax breaks for the über-wealthy. He gathered more and more patriots around him, preferably those who were already entrenched in positions of governmental authority -- From whom he could learn how to control the levers of power behind the scenes. His loyalists would do whatever he desired – As long as Turmerico granted them favors, status, privileges and the opportunity to secure even greater wealth than they already possessed … As for the poor, working and middle classes, who he was supposed to be serving as Amourrica Profunda's highest elected official -- They would be left out in the cold … Turmerico Inflammatorio's wife was named Curcuma Moulu. His daughter (from a former marriage to a Transylvanian socialite) went by the name of Francka ... Francka's husband's name was Jester Whoopy Cushy. Francka and Jester had an eight-year-old daughter named Deandra. The idea of having more children appealed to them, but they had no desire to deal with that responsibility – They were ambitious and too busy to be bothered with additional offspring ... Their number one priority, like those of the patriots, was this: To remain within the good graces of Turmerico. And to that end – They did whatever he called upon them to do.

Fortunately, enough Amourrica Profundans recognized the fact that their flawed and quasi-democratic form of government -- Was in danger of being taken from them. Consequently, the left wing of the Blues made compromises with their party's moderate center, in order to unify disparate factions, broaden the party's base -- And expand its popularity among potential new voters. But the Blues faced a formidable foe ... While campaigning (as the Red candidate for chancellor) against Giovanni and Juliana Azul (Blue candidates for chancellor) during the final year of his four-year term – Sitting Chancellor Inflammatorio's shamelessness and lack of restraint knew no bounds; *mudslinging* was a practice he relished. Giovanni and Juliana were incessantly mocked and derided by their opponent – A so-called upstart, anti-establishment outsider who'd become the unequivocal *Führer* of the Reds

… But then the candidates Azul, who'd appeared to be floundering by running an ineffective campaign -- Made an extraordinary comeback and were overwhelmingly elected by a clear majority of the Amourrica Profundan populace. The Azuls had been aided by the Blues – Who fought tooth and nail to make sure that tyrannical Inflammatorio would suffer a crushing defeat … Nonetheless, once it had become definitively clear that Turmerico had lost the election – He did not concede; he refused to make a public statement acknowledging The Azuls as the legitimately-elected chancellors-to-be.

Election officials of both the Blue and Red parties, whose job it was to oversee the vote counting processes of federal elections – Declared that the election had been the safest on record in the nation's history. Significant evidence of widespread voter fraud was found to be lacking – The actual amount of fraud proved to be so infinitesimally small, as to be completely irrelevant … Nevertheless -- Inflammatorio began to spread the lie, to his base, and to anyone else who could be conned into believing him -- That the only way the Azuls had managed to win the election was due to rampant voter fraud … *Giovanni and Juliana Azul? Not my chancellors! It's a hoax!* -- Cried the Reds, anywhere and everywhere that they could … Turmerico's supporters believed this lie – Because they were not interested in the truth. All they wanted was to have their leader back, by any means necessary, because he was a racist and a xenophobe, posing as a patriot – Who'd protect their right to own whatever kind of weapon they desired, be it civilian or military. The Reds loved their *king* who vowed to keep their country insulated, isolated and protectionist – Their *padrone* would defend them from everything that frightened and threatened them. Inflammatorio would keep the Reds safe and secure – Or so they thought.

According to the Blues -- The Reds were responsible for Amourrica Profunda's steep intellectual decline. The Reds had stopped giving credence to the universal truth of facts – Instead, they chose to believe in conspiracy theories ... The Reds were also anti-governmentalists – They believed that violence against excessively interventionist (*big*) government would be warranted in certain cases. The Reds opposed *big government* – Because they believed such a government was too *socialist*; too much about *handouts*. Devotion to the anti-governmentalist philosophy had been growing steadily during the preceding sixty years ... In defiant opposition to what they perceived to be the nefarious influence of *socialist governance*, the Reds circled their wagons and continued to unify, due to their shared belief in the traditional and universally-admired *pull-yourself-up-by-your-bootstraps* system of values.

Inflammatorio understood these anti-governmental-ists and he'd learned how to manipulate them – To hypnotize and then convert them into wholehearted supporters. Despite his vast wealth, he spoke their *no-nonsense language* and they'd bought into his deception -- Embracing everything that he stood for unconditionally … Turmerico was not a bright man -- He was sorely lacking in intellectual curiosity. But he knew what he wanted and once he was focused on obtaining whatever he was after, which in his case was unlimited power -- There was no stopping him. Once his Red followers had been sufficiently deprogrammed and made ready to do whatever he wished them to – Turmerico would carry out a fascistic coup against the Chancellors Azul and The Amourrica Profundan Governmental Apex (APGA).

The Reds owned every kind of gun – They were entirely comfortable with instilling fear into the hearts and minds of their perceived enemies. And those they despised and loathed, above all others – Happened to be the Blues … The Red males fancied themselves as being *machos* and strove to behave that way as well – The *he-man* mentality resonated strongly within their ranks. Their number one advan-tage was this: They knew how to band together to achieve solidarity – They were incredibly *tribalistic* … The Reds tended to be property owners who lived in wide-open spaces. A small fragment of the Reds could be categorized as actively engaged extremists – And that percentage was increasing. Some Red loyalists formed militias -- Which they'd utilize, as required, to carry out *vigilante justice*. Most of those groups remained local – But some militias became bolder, expanded their numbers and gained national notoriety ... And this is why: once the Reds came to realize that they'd no longer be able to win elections based on their policy-poor party platforms alone – They began to form so-called *political organizations* that would function as *domestic terror groups*. They set about brainstorming in meetings -- That most often took place in obscure, rural locations ... The largest group, that managed to achieve national notoriety – Referred to themselves as *Anarchic Rebel Patriots* (hereafter *ARPs*). The ARPs trained and strategized, readying themselves for their first public demonstration – Which would take the form of an anti-governmental protest ... The culmination of their efforts resulted in this: On the day of the inauguration of Giovanni and Juliana Azul as Co-Chancellors – The ARPs arrived *en masse* in Bruschettya-Kapitolya, Central Eastern Region. Detailed planning had been involved -- They were excessively armed and dressed in military gear. But the ARPs were up against a formidable foe. The Bruschettyan Military Protection Unit (hereafter "BMPU") was funded by the vast coffers of Bank of the Department of Defense. For that reason – Bruschettya was heavily fortified. Secondly -- BMPU had access to voluminous quantities of the following equipment: *Small arms (pistols, submachine guns, small caliber rifles, shotguns, machine guns, sniper rifles, grenade-based weapons, portable anti-material weapons); Artillery (mortars, Howitzers, rocket artillery, air defense); Vehicles (MWVs, trucks, armored vehicles, MRAPs); and Aircraft (fixed-wing aircraft, STOL, helicopters, unnamed aerial vehicles).* BMPU was armed to the teeth; their presence alone made it abundantly clear that they were ready to fight back against the ARPs -- In terms of boots on the ground, BMPU also outnumbered the ARPs by a ratio of 2:1. Once the ARPs saw what they were up against, they had no choice but to retreat – And so BMPU successfully defended its city. At least at this juncture – The Blues laughed off the ARPs, referring to them by this nickname: *Oblivious Radical Catalysts* (AKA *ORCs*).

With BMPU having effectively defeated the ARPs (ORCs) – The Co-Chancellors Azul were inaugurated, as planned. They wasted no time and got to work right off the bat … Exactly one week after their inauguration, the Azuls implemented their first executive order. By means of reports, based on statistics collected in a national survey – APGA had come to the following conclusion: That the state of mental decay affecting the Amourrica Profundan populace – Was now a matter of grave concern. Fifty-one percent of the population could no longer pronounce the name of their country – Most of the populace referred to it as *Amoolickuh Plufoonduh*. Amourrica Profunda was now so thoroughly unenlightened that the public had lost interest in classical works -- Along with their corresponding historical backdrops. Fortunately, renowned works of literature, stretching back from the present day to Old-World antiquity -- Were now being collected, stored and preserved in subterranean libraries in undisclosed locations. Those libraries were supervised by the dwindling member-ship of the Academic Learned of the Eastern and Western Regions (ALEW).

The goal of the Azul's executive order was this: To *simplify, simplify, simplify*. The executive action officially changed the name of the country from Amourrica Profunda -- To Mourrzicka (and as a direct result of that change, APGA became MGA -- The *Mourrzickan Governmental Apex*). A national marketing campaign followed to promote the nation's new name – A blurb was created and then publicized throughout the land. This blurb (some even referred to it as a *jingle*) was made available to all citizens via the internet, as well as mainstream television – And it went like this: *Mourrzicka! It's Just Gosh Darn Easier! Hell -- It's More Simpler! Gotta Love That Name! It's Got Less Syllabibbles!* ... Although enacted with good intentions, this executive order ended up being one of Giovanni and Juliana's lesser accomplishments – It was a noble effort, but frankly misguided. Simplifying the country's name -- Wouldn't solve the problem of endemic polarization. The Blues considered the executive order to be *anti-intellectual* – The Reds claimed that it *insulted their alleged collective intelligence*. But the Chancellors Azul had no other choice; something had to be done -- As literacy rates were in freefall … People had become compulsively *picture-oriented* and were wasting hours of their time being *image-obsessed* on their Tombphones. Employers had begun to complain about the reduced productivity of their workers -- Employees were now using all of their vacation time for KPD (signifying either *kooky picture days*, or *kinky picture days*). Those employees also used up all of their sick days -- And even kept calling in sick, after those sick days had been exhausted. The struggle of the workforce to cope with the adverse effects of PIM (*picture-image mania*) -- Was real. Pharmaceutical companies began to develop drugs to help those who suffered from the debilitating effects of PIM -- In doing so, the pharma firms ended up reaping huge profits, by taking advantage of a vulnerable population …

Seeing how compromise with the Blue Majority would be impossible – The Red Minority decided to secede from Mourrzicka, to form a separate country called *Neanderthalya* (which the Mourrzickan Governmental Apex would refuse to officially recognize). Neanderthalya was then founded (although illegitimately, according to MGA) in the Central, Southern, Southeastern and Northwestern Regions of Mourrzicka. This new country was immediately divided into two separate regions: *North Neanderthalya* (the Central and Northwestern Regions); and *South Neanderthalya* (the Southern and Southeastern Regions). Directly after the founding of Neanderthalya, due to their shared ideological principles -- The Red Minority formally joined with the ARPs; in other words, the Reds became Anarchic Rebel Patriots. The party name of Red was then retired and relegated to history -- The ARPs were now a combined political party and domestic terrorist organization. Due to the existence of this newly formed union – The ARPs gained a tremendous cache of guns and weaponry as well. The ARPs promptly began to train their massive influx of new members – Their combined forces studied the latest military tactics used by Old-World neo-fascistic armies, to develop strategies for future victories. So what if BMPU wagged its finger at the ARPs and compared their methods -- To those of banana republics and tinpot dictators? The ARPs would have the last laugh now – It was just a matter of time before they conquered both BMPU and the Blues. As the ARPs now had an enormous army at their disposal -- Absolute power and its concomitant corruption would be theirs for the taking ...

One of the first governmental actions taken by the ARPs, within their newly subjugated Neanderthalyan territories, was the indoctrination of children – Who'd receive military training and be instilled with the values of that culture, to prepare them for future battles against any hostile faction that decided to invade Neanderthalya. This indoctrination included having all children, ages six to eighteen, be subject to mandatory brainwashing, during certain designated school days -- At various local chapters of The Center for Mandatory Anarchic Rebel Thought ("CMART") throughout North and South Neanderthalya. The headquarters of CMART were located in the city of Bear Mace -- On the southeastern edge (of the Northwestern Region) of North Neanderthalya. The Administrative Headquarters of The ARPs (hereafter "ARPAH") that managed all of the governmental services for both North and South Neanderthalya – Were also located in the city of Bear Mace.

Predictably, although not officially (and in strained cooperation with North Neanderthalya) South Neanderthalya would ultimately function as its own Evilangelist theocracy. Consequently, citizens' allegiance to Evilangelism in South Neanderthalya – Would then be rigorously enforced ... By the time that Amourrica Profunda's name had been changed to that of Mourrzicka, the Evilangelists had dispensed with archaic *Jah-Hee-Zeus;* they now worshipped a terrifying one-eyed deity -- Known as *Cyclopxia Christi.* The city of Branyghan, in the Sub-Region of Eurekana, South Neanderthalya -- Was the spiritual home of Cyclopxia Christi. It had been determined by the Branyghan Regional Apex *(BRA)* that pilgrimages once every six months to Branyghan -- Would be compulsory for both North and South Neanderthalyan Evilangelists ... Funds for South Neanderthalya's coffers -- Were donated by the thousands who regularly attended Evilangelist Megafortress services. Fifty percent of those dona-tions were then sent to the ARP Administrative Headquarters ["ARPAH"] in North Neanderthalya – To discourage any potentially destabilizing inter-nal conflicts between competing religious factions. The other fifty percent of the donations were used to reinforce Neanderthalya's military readiness – To protect it from possible attacks by mercenaries from the majority Blue Eastern and Western Regions ... The Blues did not believe in engaging in armed conflict with any of their fellow citizens (either Neanderthalyan or Mourrzickan) – Unless solutions, by means of dialogue and diplomacy, became impossible to attain. The Blues claimed that they wanted to help their ARP brethren – The ARPs sus-pected that the Blues had ulterior motives. The ARPs would never trust the Blues and the Blues didn't trust the ARPs either – The Blues only wanted to save the ARPs, from what they viewed as being the ARPs' dedication to ignorance and absurdity.

The largest Evilangelist Megafortress in Neanderthalya (and in Mourrzicka as well) -- Was called Voldemordor and was located in Branyghan. Voldemordor also functioned as a seat of government for the Branyghan Regional Apex (*BRA*). The mega-Megafortress that was Voldemordor -- Was protected by state-of-the-art, mechanized steel doors, shutters and gates. Every evening at sundown, those steel doors, shutters and gates would slam shut, just as an undesirable element of the local population (AKA *agitators*) – Would gather outside of Voldemordor to dance, howl at the moon and shoot their guns into the air. As the agitators saw it, they were causing no harm – They were merely letting off some steam. BRA let them be, for the time being. Thanks to the security provided by Voldemordor's steel doors, shutters and gates, the unruly locals could have their fun – Without BRA having to confiscate their weapons. However, what BRA failed to recognize was this: that the behavior of the agitators was a harbinger of deadlier actions to come -- That would eventually flower into ongoing internecine conflicts throughout South Neanderthalya (and eventually North Neanderthalya as well) … All Neanderthalyans, from both the North and the South

-- Would continue to devolve, due to their embrace of the following: The philosophy and practices of (1) militias; (2) conspiracy theorists; and (3) delusional survivalist cults -- From all over the Blue Green Planet.

CONCEAL AND CARRY: THE MUSICAL

PAMM AND REMMY PROMOTE THEIR NEW PROJECT

Pamm Demmyck and Remmy Dessyvyr were sitting in an office on the top floor of a skyscraper -- In the Sanctuary City of Megalopola, Megajorcka, Northeastern Region, Mourrzicka, God-Wanna, Blue Green Planet. They were waiting to meet with a producer who they hoped would turn their latest project, "Conceal and Carry: The Musical", into a big hit -- In Megalopola's nationally renowned theatrical district of Triplethreat. The book and lyrics were written by Pamm – The music was composed by Remmy. Remmy had no musical training – But she was resourceful and found a way to "borrow" from the composers of obscure, unsuccessful "way-off-Triplethreat" musicals. As a part of the song writing process – Remmy had the keys of all of the appropriated melodies changed from major to minor (or vice versa); Pamm then provided new lyrics. Remmy hired musicians, from all over the Blue Green Planet, who could play diverse styles of percussion – Along with brass, flutes, gongs, wind chimes, maracas, cymbals, castanets, tambourines and xylophones. Most of the musicians were great improvisers -- Remmy would command them to "play blue!", "play red!" or "play yellow!"; they'd immediately understand what she wanted them to produce for her. And Remmy's palette was diverse; she was not afraid of nuance -- Sometimes she'd also yell out "play orange!", "play purple! or "play brown!" Then the instrumentalists would offer up some riffs and Remmy would approve or disapprove -- In the manner of a decadent empress from Old-World antiquity, with a thumbs up or a thumbs down … Or she'd nod her head, up and down -- Wearing a big smile … Or she'd shake her head from side to side, sporting a frown – As if she was an anger emoji … Remmy was lucky to have these musicians as collaborators, who ultimately provided her with polished melodies and a complete score. For the most part – Remmy functioned as an amateur conductor and minimally as a composer. That being the case -- The players acted shrewdly, as they were not going to be taken advantage of. They created most of the music, while being paid for their time – On the condition that they'd be given compositional credits, in the event that the show went on to become a hit.

Pamm and Remmy were nervous as they waited, but also excited … No risk – No reward! So much was riding on this – They were eager to make a big leap forward with their careers, by finding success with this venture … And it turned out that Pamm and Remmy were lucky – The Megalopolan producer in question decided to take on their project. It would be produced in the Hawthorne Johnson Theatre in the Triplethreat district. The show eventually opened to good reviews, and it looked as if it would run for months – If not years! … But then one day, tragedy struck – A militia consisting of "Anarchic Rebel Patriots" ("ARPs") had traveled from Neanderthalya to Megalopala to create havoc. The goal of their troops was this: To commit acts of domestic terrorism … Bombs were set off by the ARPs at several theatres in the Triplethreat district – The Hawthorne Johnson Theatre was among the targets and suffered extensive damage. Fortunately, there were fewer casualties than expected, since for some unknown reason -- The ARPs had executed their attack during daylight hours, missing the evening theatre crowds in the process … "Conceal And Carry: The Musical" had to be shut down, until the theatre could either be repaired -- Or another space could be secured in which to house the production.

Ultimately – A worst-case scenario ended up occurring. After the bombings had been carried out, the contingent of ARPs traveled to Bruschettya-Kapitolya,

Central Eastern Region, Mourrzicka – The second sanctuary city that lay in their sights. As it turned out, the botched execution of their plan in Triplethreat was just a dress rehearsal – Once in Bruschettya, the ARP militia was joined by an influx of thousands of ARP soldiers; their combined forces then carried out a coup and declared themselves to be the new leaders of Mourrzicka. The BMPU ("Bruschettyan Military Protection Unit") proved to be no match for the newly armed, expanded, retrained and reorganized ARPs – BMPU promptly surrendered, after realizing that they'd lose the battle and suffer catastrophic losses ... Once the coup had been achieved, the ARPs swiftly issued a proclamation (broadcast live to the entire nation) -- Which stated the following: "From this day forward -- Mourrzicka will be known as Isolamicka. Compliance is compulsory -- That is all." The Mourrzickan Governmental Apex (MGA) was then promptly renamed IGA -- The "Isolamickan Governmental Apex" ... IGA banned all forms of creative expression straight away -- IGA hated the arts. From that point forward – Creativity, in all of its myriad genres, would be forced underground. Anyone who was found using their creative agency to make art would be abducted – And most likely never heard from again. Writers, thinkers, academics, journalists and philosophers started disappearing via kidnappings – To face detention, torture and in some cases execution. Print media outlets were either heavily censored or *shut down completely. Theatres and musical venues were shuttered, visual art in museums was destroyed and music was silenced ... Life everywhere in what was now Isolamicka -- Took on a paranoid hue ...*

Giovanni Azul, along with his wife and co-chancellor Juliana -- Were captured by the ARPs. They were then deported to the headquarters of CMART in Bear Mace, Northwestern Region (Neanderthalya), Isolamicka – Where they would be brainwashed and kept as prisoners ... Turmerico Inflammatorio was subsequently installed by the ARPs as the authoritarian ruler of Isolamicka ... Evilangelists from everywhere in Isolamicka – Rejoiced upon hearing that Inflammatorio had been newly enthroned as their czar ... Naturally, the Blues were traumatized by Turmerico's coronation, as well as by the kidnapping of the Azuls – But they would not be stopped by sadness; there was no time to waste. They began to fortify their sanctuary cities in the Eastern and Western regions ... Pamm and Remmy remained in Megalopola where they connected with its underground culture – Which expeditiously transformed itself into the Anti-Isolamickan Resistance, in which Pamm and Remmy were both active participants ... Although the two of them didn't realize it, Pamm Demmyck and Remmy Dessyvyr were the reigning Cassandras of their time, having foreseen in their dreams -- The transformation of Mourrzicka into Isolamicka ...

Conceal and Carry: The Musical
[The Story of Trudy True-Vada]
Book and Lyrics by Pamm Demmyck
Music by Remmy Dessyvyr
[With additional music provided by:
Ms. Dessyvyr's collaborators --
Who did most of the work]

Synopsis of *Conceal and Carry: The Musical*

The protagonist, Trudy True-Vada -- Grew up in the rough-and-tumble city of Fuente de la Juventud, in the Subtropical Maroon-Fuchsia Sub-Region of Whorelandya, Southeastern Region (in what was then Amourrica Profunda). As soon as Trudy turned twenty-one – She registered for a conceal-and-carry permit. Because instead of realizing her show business dreams in the old-fashioned way (through tenacity and hard work) – She had something much more audacious in mind. Ever since her childhood, she'd been planning on taking advantage of Whorelandya's relaxed gun laws and regulations – So that she could shoot down anyone who decided to *get in her way*, knowing that she'd face no consequences. She would *stand her ground* ... No one was going to stop Trudy from getting her big break -- Even if she didn't have any talent. All of the local agents and managers that she'd encountered thus far, who could have helped her to make headway in the business – Bluntly dismissed her, each with their own version of the following: *We don't think you have what it takes to succeed in show business and we're going to do our damned-est to make sure that you never sing and dance for a single human being – For as long as ye shall live …* She would never forgive them for their utter lack of support -- For trying to prevent her from achieving her dreams. She would make them pay for the way that they'd treated her …

AN EXCERPT FROM TRUDY TRUE-VADA'S OPENING MONOLOGUE

[*From Conceal and Carry: The Musical*]

TRUDY: I JES WUNTS TO GET UP THERE AND DO SOME SINGIN AND DANCIN! I AIN'T TRYIN TO PAINT NO SISTINE CHAPEL! I KNOW THE TRUTH ABOUT WHAT I IS! I AIN'T AFEARED UH BEIN ALL VILE AND CRUDE … I AIN'T AFEARED UH DOIN NO LOWEST COMMON DENOMINATION … SO THAT'S WHAT I'LL BE GITTIN UP TO, TO LIVE MY DREAM – I'LL GO NUKYUHLUR AND BECOME THE MOST FAMOUS ENTURTAYNUR THE WHIRLD'S DONE EVER KNOWED!

On the surface, Trudy had a charming folksiness about her – She could connect with, and endear herself to, everyday people. She put on no airs – She alienated no one … But beneath her charismatic exterior, it was the spirit of her ancestors that drove her -- Those being

the virulently, vindictive Whorelandyan plantation mis-
tresses, who'd worked their evil magic during a tragic
time in Amourrica Profundan history ... Similarly to her
forbears, Trudy knew how to sugar coat her venom
-- That was her true talent that emboldened her and
lit the fire of her ambition. Through sheer persistence
and in spite of her questionable ability, Trudy became
a major movie star – She carved out a career niche
for herself as an *underdog / anti-heroine* type. She
eventually became a household word throughout
Isolamicka – But would be particularly beloved in both
North and South Neanderthalya ...

THE STORY OF TRUDY TRUE-VADA (A POEM)

She was the bad girl
With a heart of ice
Who lived in a trailer
At the end of a dead-end road
In a part of town
Bordering on them thar
Dark piney woods
Which you'd best not go into
Alone at night

But the same quality that made her popular with
moviegoers – Also made her real life very difficult.
Long-term relationships challenged her and eventually became impossible for her to maintain. She

broke the hearts of her lovers with her brutal honesty – That seemed to erupt from her spontaneously, with no apparent forethought. She paid dearly for her inability to control that shortcoming -- The men that she wounded moved on without hesitation. And who could blame them, for seeking out love, light, stability and rationality elsewhere … Eventually, Trudy was consumed by her demons -- Which ate away at her soul and contributed to her prolonged mental and physical deterioration. Hers was a slow decline and a creeping death – That she'd brought upon herself. Near the end of her life, Trudy True-Vada was awarded the Gym Part-Fascism Anti-Humanitarian Award by the Isolamickan Hieronymus Boscar Academy of Blatant Anti-Artistick Compromise. But the recognition gave her little solace -- As by that time her disillusionment with life had become so extreme that rewards meant nothing to her … Since childhood, she'd only been posing as a church-going Lutheran. Per her final wishes -- She chose to be cremated on a Viking funeral pyre. She'd always felt an affinity, as well as respect -- For the Old-World northern pagan cultures and their mythologies. She viewed the people of those societies (specifically, the men) as having been aggressive and beastly predators -- Marauders, warmongers, plunderers, looters, arsonists and rapists. She considered the *Vikings*, as she imagined them -- To be equivalent to the idea of an *Aryan race*. Hence -- She was a firm believer in the superiority of Caucasians

… People of color were taking over the continent of God-Wanna, the Old-World and the rest of the Blue Green Planet as well – And knowing that (especially without being able to admit it) made her *mad as hell* … In the years following her death, Trudy True-Vada became a legend, known for her monumental contributions to the overarching tradition of anti-intellectual aesthetics -- That were a predominant feature of Isolamickan culture …

FRANCKA INFLAMMATORIO
AND
TURMERICO INFLAMMATORIO

Francka Inflammatorio lay down on her bed, in the second-floor master suite of the Off-White House, 6666 Transylvania Avenue, Bruschettya-Kapitolya, Central Eastern Region, Isolamicka, God-Wanna, Blue Green Planet. She had a rare evening of downtime ahead of her and was looking forward some overdue relaxation … She became pensive and started to think about her father, Turmerico Inflammatorio, who she adored and worshipped – And how he'd made it, against all odds, in the pursuit of dubious ventures (even though going down such a path had been completely unnecessary for him, as he'd inherited hundreds of millions of dollars from his father).

Once upon a time, in a previous chapter of her life (in what was then Amourrica Profunda) Turmerico's wife, Curcuma Moulu -- Loved to hang out with GB men (AKA the GB portion of LGBTQIA; AKA "gay and bisexual men"). She had no regrets about her pre-Turmerican years as a charismatic fag hag. Although there were those who said that she'd wasted years of her life being a party girl, by spending too many wild nights in anti-heteronormative discos and clubs -- Turmerico decided to overlook that character flaw. He married her and supported her financially for the rest of their life together ... He was lucky to have her by his side – It was Curcuma who helped Turmerico to establish his orange ass hair business (hereafter "OAH"). As his body produced OAH at a highly prolific rate -- Turmerico would finally capitalize on that resource and go full steam ahead with spinning OAH into gold ... In that regard, Curcuma was a woman with a plan; one day, she came home after a busy day of shopping – And presented her husband with a surprise: A high-pressure hose, which he would use to clean his intergluteal cleft. Curcuma had found out about this item from one of her Old-World GB connections -- It was the kind of high-pressure hose that was commonly used by men who had sex with men. It originated in an Old-World, democratically socialist, Reign-Beau-flag-laden city in a part of Mutter Erde -- Where GB men enjoyed shame-free sexual decadence. Thanks to Curcuma's discovery of this new method of personal hygiene for Turmerico – His OAH would be converted into the raw material that would eventually become the foundation of Turmerico's latest business venture ... In the early days of their partnership, Curcuma used OAH to produce an abundance of durable orange yarn – She worked tirelessly, as if she was Sleeping Beauty spinning away at her spindle. Her creation of OAH yarn was accomplished in a special arts and crafts room -- In the penthouse of Turmerican Tower, Megalopola, Megajorcka. After Turmerico's cleaning (along with some minimal douching), drying and orange ass-hair shaving -- Curcuma would gather up all of the OAH and then triple-wash it with gusto. She was not squeamish; this was nothing, compared to what she'd had to endure in the Old-World -- Shoveling pig manure for days on end, on the farm where she'd been raised ...

Inflammatorio trusted Curcuma completely and allowed her to run the entire enterprise. Ultimately, thanks to Curcuma's business savvy – The production of OAH was ramped up and then transformed into consumer-ready merchandise. That merchandise included curtains, potholders, dishtowels, doormats, yoga mats, shower mats – And even windbreakers! Those products were then distributed to Isolamickan consumer outlets – Like Fall of Civilization-Mart, Home Despot and Lowbrows – Chain stores that were controlled by billionaires and filled with planet-destroying products ... Despite Turmerico's body *having the ability to produce plenteous quantities of OAH -- More employees, whose specialized skills would be dedicated to the ever-increasing production of OAH, would have to be hired (in order to accommodate rising consumer demand). Namely, hundreds of scientists and their assistants, from that point on – Would be responsible for overseeing the fabrication of orange ass hair (going forward, OAH would be derived from stem cell tissue) ... Once those new and highly skilled professionals had been installed and the business was growing and thriving as a result – Inflammatorio's services as a "guinea pig" would no longer be required ... Production levels soon surpassed targets forecast by operations management – Leading to the greenlighting of construction of additional plants, laboratories and warehouses all over Isolamicka. Yes, Turmerico's achievement had been built on a disgusting practice – But now, all of its unsavory elements had finally been laundered and the enterprise had been transformed into one that was sparkling clean ..."Turmerican Wonder Fabric" (the brand name) ultimately became available everywhere and was unwittingly beloved by a majority of the population of the Blue Green Planet ...*

The Evilangelists, who devotedly followed Turmerico, as if he were Cyclopxia Christi himself – Made no objections to the way that OAH was produced. They had no problem with how this work was being done, even though they considered human embryonic stem cell ["HESC"] research to be unethical -- Since the harvesting of stem cells destroyed embryos, which went against their core, pro-life values. They accepted the utilization of stem cell tissue, as being a necessary part of the process of creating OAH -- Because they were hypocritical predatory capitalists, as well as loyal cult members who loved money, the true golden idol of Evilangelism ... Being aware that they comprised an important part of Turmerico's base – They wanted to make sure that they would not be forgotten by Signore Inflammatorio when he needed their support. The only reason that the Evilangelists remained an enthusiastic segment of Turmerico's base -- Was so they could get what they wanted, once he was swept back into power along with the ARPs ... However, the day finally came along – When things started to go downhill, for the following reason: Inflammatorio was a cheap bastard who underpaid his employees and treated them poorly. They'd started to publicly protest the miserable conditions under which they labored. Turmerico was stubborn, to the point of self-sabotage; he refused to raise the wages of his employees -- Even though he possessed vast personal resources, which would have easily made such a move possible. And so, his workers staged strikes, to demand higher wages and improved benefits. But when their appeals were

*ignored, because Inflammatorio refused to budge –
They walked out of their workplaces, never to return
… Turmerico was then forced to advertise for more
employees, but people were no longer interested
in working for him -- Because they knew that they
would not be paid a living wage; they realized that
their work would not be valued. As Inflammatorio
had trouble finding new workers who'd accept the
humiliation of being paid paltry wages -- It wasn't
long before Turmerican Wonder Fabric, and all of the
products that were derived from it, stopped being
produced. Tumerico's factories, laboratories and
warehouses, wherever they were located -- Were
shuttered and abandoned. His empty plants wound
up being covered with graffiti -- That was splattered
all over the buildings, randomly and often in brilliant
color …*

As a child, Turmerico had always told Francka:
*HOW MANY TIMES DO I HAVE TO TELL YOU TO HIDE
ALL OF YOUR UNDECLARED INCOME AND ILL-
GOTTEN GAINS -- IN OFFSHORE BANK ACCOUNTS!*
He'd also encourage her to … *SHOOT FROM THE HIP!
SAY WHAT THE FUCK YOU WANT, DO WHAT THE FUCK
YOU WANT AND FUCK WHAT ANYONE THINKS! JUST
STEAMROLL OVER EVERYONE! OVERHWHELM THEM
WITH RELENTLESS AUDACITY AND NEVER LOOK BACK
…* Her father had trained her to be a ruthless pred-
atory capitalist princess, expert at stealing taxpayer

dollars, from what he referred to as "a clueless populace". In this way – Francka was able to pull the levers of power in the administration of an oligarchy-plutocracy-kleptocracy – Otherwise known as either a hybrid authoritarian regime, or an anocracy... *WHETHER IT'S AN ILLIBERAL DEMOCRACY OR A FASCIST DICTATORSHIP – WHATEVER PAYS THE BEST, WILL BE BEST, SO THAT WE CAN LAUGH ALL THE WAY TO THE BANK – Francka would constantly remind herself* ... Thoughts like those would consume her during her daily meditation sessions (although such notions had to be immediately dispelled, in order to focus on her breathing). For she was absolutely committed to her practice of Machiavellian Mindfulness – A discipline that would aid her in blooming like an evil flower, the goal being to secure her place upon the throne of Absolute Power ...

Life was good at the Off-White House for Francka, as it was for her two vampire brothers, Nefarick and Turmerico Jr. -- With whom she was making a killing in their Blissful Bower of Nepotism. Yes, they'd made their Faustian bargains -- But did this make them evil? It most certainly did – Life was too short to play fair and that was the only excuse they needed to lie, cheat and steal their way to success ... The three of them, who referred to themselves as the *Unholie Trynytie* -- Could care less if they turned *The Blue Green Planet (BGP)* into a fiery, hellish landscape, due to their ruthless actions … Francka had a plaque hanging on the wall -- In front of her home office desk, that read: ASTRONOMICAL OIL PROFITS (AN INDUSTRY IN WHICH THE INFLAMMATORIO FAMILY IS HEAVILY INVESTED) CREATE THE CAPITAL REQUIRED TO FINANCE THE UPKEEP OF OUR INNUMERABLE REAL ESTATE HOLDINGS! The ultimate goal that the Unholie Trynytie sought to accomplish – Was to destroy all obstacles to power that lay in its path and for its three members to be the best predatory capitalists ever (AKA "BPCEs") in their exclusive and top-secret BPCE Club!

All of the rooms inside of the Off-White House were painted black, because the only kind of arts that Daddy Turmerico chose to patronize – Were the Dark Arts. There was no discernible difference between *9 to 5 Turmerico* and *Off-Hours Inflammatorio* -- He was depraved, deranged and demented 24-7. And Francka was his not-so-sweet little sorceress … Together, under the guidance of her Father and with the help of her brothers – Francka was turning Isolamicka into a pariah nation. And the most import-ant step, in making this happen – Was taxing the hell out of the 99 percent and subsequently lining the pockets of the 1 percent. So what if the lower and middle classes were on the brink of starvation and regularly marching through the streets with torches and pitchforks? That kind of drama was exhilarating for Turmerico -- Who reveled in any kind of attention, negative or otherwise … And in the unlikely event that the masses' hatred (that was directed towards him constantly) became too much for him to bear -- He could always escape to his compound, Guillaume-Barr-A-Lago, in the Subtropical Maroon Fuchsia Sub-Region of Whorelandya. Guillaume-Barr-A-Lago had recently been fortified with state-of-the-art, mechanized steel doors, shutters and gates – It was a home away from home! 6666 Transylvania Avenue had also been newly secured – It was well-protected by an Evilangelist militia that provided round-the-clock service to deal with any socialist rabblerousers …

FRANCKA AND DEANDRA

As for Francka's eight-year-old daughter Deandra – Francka didn't even pretend to love her. And honestly, Deandra didn't need her mother – As she was being raised by Ioana (pronounced *Eye-Yo-Wanna*) a Transylvanian governess. Francka was too busy to be a mother -- She didn't have the energy for all of that. Every moment of the day was dedicated to growing her business -- So that her father Turmerico would be proud of her. Her demanding and exhausting workdays were spent screaming at people that she considered to be idiots -- Specifically, those who toiled in her sweatshops in the impoverished Southeastern Tropical Lands of a Communist Region

Far Away to the East. Her internationally dispersed management teams lived in fear of their Doom meetings with notoriously volatile Francka ... Deep down, in a way that she could barely access, Francka probably loved her daughter Deandra. But on a typically busy and stressful day -- Francka would just as soon have punched her. Fortunately -- Ioana was able to protect Deandra from Francka's infrequent and toxically dysfunctional attempts at bonding ...

Then one late afternoon, when Ioana had the day off, Francka showed up out of the blue for a rare moment of family time – Naturally, Deandra wanted nothing to do with her Mommy, especially with her having turned up so unexpectedly ... When Francka knocked on the door of Deandra's lavishly appointed second-floor bedroom (which was adjacent to Francka's and Jester Whoopy Cushy's master suite) Deandra reluctantly opened the door and told her to enter. Francka came into the room wearing a horrendously inauthentic smile and over-enthusiastically proclaimed: *HELLO!* Deandra responded by unceremoniously sticking out her tongue – With a hostile look on her face. In that moment, Francka decided that her daughter would have to be punished.

Francka: C'MON YOUNG LADY! WE'RE GOING FOR A DRIVE!

They drove southward, on the interstate, then the local highway -- Before exiting onto the main street of some small country town. They then drove through that municipality -- Until they reached the southern edge of the village. At that point, Francka turned to the left -- And onto a dark, winding road with no streetlights. They cruised onward for a couple of miles -- They were now truly out in the middle of nowhere. They then turned right, onto an unmarked dirt road that ran through an evergreen forest – And continued for a quarter of a mile. Francka pulled over, parked the car and turned off the ignition – She then barked at her daughter:

Francka: GET OUT OF THIS CAR RIGHT NOW -- YOU UNGRATEFUL SPOILED BRAT!

Francka then pulled two flashlights from out of her Pravda bag and handed one of them to Deandra, telling her sternly: TURN IT ON NOW … They'd arrived at a clearing where there was nothing but a rusty metal trash can, in the center of a bare-dirt open space – With a bunch of logs scattered haphazardly nearby. Francka threw down her bag and started tossing the logs -- Into the rusty trash can. She then collected some dry kindling and threw it on top of the logs. She then retrieved some lighter fluid and matches from her Pravda bag and ignited the contents of the trash can. They waited a few minutes for the flames to grow … Francka had also brought a brown paper grocery bag along with her -- Deandra had no idea what was in it. After a couple of more minutes, Francka looked at Deandra with a wicked smile on her face – And then pulled a crumpled-up piece of paper out of the brown paper bag...

Francka: (viciously sarcastic) Look what we've got here! Your refrigerator drawings! Well -- Mommy's going to teach you a lesson now! Because no daughter of mine is going to grow up, only to fritter her life away -- Drawing pretty little pictures! Because you're going to be a ruthless predatory capitalist -- Just like your Mommy! And I'm going to be so proud of you! You're going to burn down the Sud-Amourrica Profundan Rainforest – That's my wish for you, because that's what people like us do! And speaking of killing trees – Here we go! WE'WE GOING TO BUWN UP AWW OF YOW WEFWIGEAWATOW DWAWINGS!

Francka proceeded to empty the paper grocery bag, containing all of her daughter's crumpled up drawings -- Into the flaming trash can ... She started to laugh, at first with delight, then more aggressively -- Until she was cackling like a lunatic ... Deandra was alarmed, then frightened – Before settling into shock ... After Francka decided that enough time had passed for Deandra's drawings to be fully incinerated – She looked at her daughter, with an expression of extreme faux-pity and told her that it was time to go. Francka did not extinguish the flames -- She let them *continue to burn … Deandra followed her mother back to the car, as if she was an automaton; she kept quiet, because she had a feeling that her survival was at stake -- And that hushing up would serve her best in that instance.*

Francka and Deandra drove home in silence. Upon their return to the Off-White House -- Deandra jumped out of the car, ran inside and then upstairs. She slammed the door of her bedroom and then locked it … Francka parked the car outside in the drive-through *portico*. After killing the engine, she leapt out and then followed right after Deandra – Climbing two stairs at a time, in a menacing, vampiric way … She began knocking on Deandra's door while speaking loudly and over-enunciating.

Francka: YOU'D BETTER OPEN THIS DOOR RIGHT NOW, YOUNG LADY – OR I'LL BREAK IT DOWN!

Deandra: MOMMY'S A MONSTER! MOMMY'S A MONSTER! MOMMY'S A MONSTER! MOMMY'S A MONSTER!

Francka's fury escalated and she broke down the door as promised. She walked over to the window across from the end of Deandra's bed – And opened it, in no time flat. She then hustled over to Deandra, picked her up by her ankles and held her upside down -- Just outside of the second-floor bedroom window, for one minute … To simultaneously teach her a lesson and traumatize her for life … After this, Francka brought Deandra back inside, threw her down on the bed and slapped her face repeatedly – Oblivious to her daughter's sobbing and wailing … Francka then left the room and marched downstairs to make herself a cocktail – She had to chill out. She needed a breather and was going to have a little fun tonight, because her hubbie Jester, who worked for Turmerico – Was on yet another business trip, making deals with some tinpot crackpot dictator from a banana republic (that masqueraded itself as an *emerging nation*) … Time to let her hair down! And then she danced her way into the living room, in the Wicked Wing of the West of the Off-White House. She threw back a Stoli screwdriver, turned up *Kung Fu Fighting* full blast, dimmed the lights – And then boogied underneath a disco ball that was spinning around above her head. She gyrated with wild abandon …

BURN BABY BURN DISCO INFERNO! Francka shrieked -- As she threw her arms up in the air and broke out her best dance moves …

Deandra lay on her bed – Staring at the ceiling. She was very upset, but gradually calmed down – She was stronger than she gave herself credit for. She would get through this … That night, Deandra made a vow -- To always do the opposite of whatever Mommy told her. Mommy would never be the one who was going to decide how Deandra lived her life -- Deandra would determine that for herself … The next day, it was back to business-as-usual for Francka: If Deandra couldn't deal with what Mommy had done to her, too bad -- Mommy could care less … Francka's work occupied her constantly. She was consumed with overseeing the production of fake, sweatshop-labor-produced designer handbags – That looked completely authentic. It gave her a tremendous thrill to inflate the retail value of that merchandise and then pawn it off onto unsuspecting consumers … *Busy, busy, busy!*

THE OBSCURE LIFE OF SUNNIE'S BROTHER BOBBIE

Sunnie Deelite's older brother Bobbie was driving down a dark road – Lined with tall, silver-blue evergreen trees on both sides. He was headed northward in Heliotrope Sub-Region, Northwestern Region (Neanderthalya), Isolamicka -- It was a cool and refreshing autumn evening and Bobbie felt surprisingly relaxed … Bobbie left home after graduating from high school – He was eighteen at the time; Sunnie was thirteen. Early on, he knew that he'd have to leave his family; he'd taken off, because he'd seen the writing on the wall, in terms of who he'd become – Were he to fall under the influence of his parents and their world. By raising him as they did, Bobbie's parents were only doing what they thought was *right* – But he refused to tolerate their values (that they subjected him to constantly) as those values were at odds with his ... Bobbie was not affiliated with any political party – He was an *independent*; the current-day Isolamickans were descended from a long line of Amourrica Profundan *individualists*. During Bobbie's Amourrica Profundan adolescence -- Mother and Father had both been centrists – Politically, Mother was Blue-Purple and Father was Red-Purple (Mom leaned progressive and Dad leaned conservative).

As a result of his ongoing indoctrination, imparted upon him by his parents -- Bobbie felt like he was being suffocated. He would never acquiesce to carving out the respectable future that his parents had envisioned for him. All they had to offer him, as far as Bobbie was concerned, was a dream of placid conformity -- That they'd been pushing on him ever since he was a little boy. Was he going to get a job with benefits? Would he adhere to practices and obligations, expected by the gatekeepers of outmoded social and cultural institutions -- As his parents had done? No way ... Objectively speaking – He could see how certain establishment beacons lit the way for the masses and worked for the good of society as a whole. But guiding lights of that nature didn't work for him and so he moved on ... Bobbie was raised in Small City -- In the western part of Blue-Purple Sub-Region, Northeastern Region (in what was then Amourrica Profunda). During his childhood and adolescence, he'd identified with Sunnie – They'd shared an irreverent sense of humor, as well as interests in writing, music, books and theatre. Their bond was strong – But one that could be forsaken; there was no way that Bobbie was going to continue living under the same roof as that of their parents. The connection to his family, or at least to his immediate, biological family -- Had to be sacrificed …

Bobbie had never expressed any interest in attending college – What would he learn there? That experience wouldn't teach him any real-world skills. To survive, as well as thrive, he chose to *work with the workers* … He found employment in restaurants, first as a busboy, then as a waiter, a barback and finally as a bartender. And while that kind of work was tolerable for him – He was also willing to flirt with the underworld if that made his life easier. ANYTHING WAS BETTER THAN WORKING FOR THE MAN … And so he became a drug dealer; he adopted modes of behavior that would help him to prosper within that domain – Which ended up being lucrative for him. He was careful and discreet -- He kept a low profile. He lived only in rural areas and always strove to blend in with the locals. Although he was not a people person per se – He appeared to be *easy-going*; over the years, he'd developed the ability to disguise his occasionally pernicious moods. Be it fear, anger, anxiety, rage, malaise, sadness or depression – He kept a lid on all of that; his temperament appeared to be unflappable … He drove a refurbished 1977 pine green Chevy Nova and loved to cruise through evergreen areas where there was plenty of fresh air – Along with hills, valleys, rivers and waterfalls. He wore hoodies, blue jeans, camouflage pants and T-shirts, olive-green military fatigues, hiking boots and ski caps. He favored T-shirts with logos that identified him as a regular guy -- Logos representing hard rock and heavy metal bands, popular beers and the Isolamickan flag ... Not only did he wear many hats, but also many masks, because he knew that he had to – His façade would be the key to his survival ...

As he was driving, Bobbie was flipping through the dial, looking for a radio station with good reception – When a man darted out from the pine forest on the right and ran up to the side of the road. The man was flagging him down frantically ... Yes, it was nighttime and he was in the middle of nowhere, but Bobbie knew how to deal with country folk and besides – He always carried a weapon. Initially, in his early adulthood, he hadn't been a fan of guns -- But he was pragmatic. The decision that he'd made to live with firearms – Had been conscious and pre-meditated. He often reminded himself: *I only use these for self-protection -- And only when I feel threatened* ... He pulled over and put his car in park on the shoulder of the road. He observed Frantic Man advancing towards his vehicle. *What am I getting myself into?*

-- Bobbie thought to himself, before rolling down the passenger side window a crack …

Bobbie: (*suspiciously*) Are you all right?

Frantic Man: (*agitated*) No! I mean – I don't know!

Bobbie: (*calmly*) What's going on?

Frantic Man: I've just witnessed the most terrifying event!

Bobbie: *(upbeat yet skeptical)* And what's your name?

Frantic Man: Chester -- Brother. And yours?

Bobbie: Bobbie …

Bobbie rolls down the passenger side window. Bobbie offers his fist -- For a fist bump. Chester reciprocates.

Bobbie: How can I help you?

Chester: (*nervously*) You have to see what I've seen! We're not far from the action – I'll take you there! There's a dirt road about half a mile back … If you don't mind, we'll drive back there, park your car so that no one can see it from the road – And then we'll walk for about three-quarters of a mile. Don't worry, it'll be perfectly safe -- I know the area …

Bobbie: (*warily*) What are we going to see?

Chester: (*in earnest*) I'm not one hundred percent sure, exactly what's going on at this gathering, but everything that I've seen so far leads me to believe – That it's some kind of cult … I keep an eye out for unusual types who move into this locale -- These people are involved in something peculiar … This last time, while I was watching them from afar -- I began to get a bad feeling; I can't explain it! All I know is that the hair stood up on the back of my neck and I got goosebumps! You'll see when we get there and then you can decide for yourself …

Bobbie: (*evenly yet assertively*) Well frankly, Chester – Why should I trust you? How do I know that you're good for your word? How do I know that you're not a part of this sect yourself? Are you leading me into a dangerous situation? Are you trying to lure me into a trap?

Chester: (*acquiescing*) Okay then – I'll put my cards on the table. I did used to be a member of this cult -- I left about a month ago when things started to get strange … I swear in the name of Cyclopxia Christi that what I'm telling you now is the truth! (*sotto voce*) I have to gather evidence and I need you to be a witness – I'm looking to build a credible case that I can take to the county officials. What these people are doing at their ceremonies needs to be brought out into the light of day!

Bobbie: (*matter-of-factly*) Did you take any photos that you could use as evidence?

Chester: No, but that's what I'd like both of us to do -- Yes, that's what we'll do; take pictures with our phones … (*disturbingly, in a low voice*) I need someone who'll have backup photos -- In case something happens to me. Heaven forbid that be the case, but …

Bobbie turns his face away from Chester and looks straight ahead through the windshield. He obviously wants as little to do with the local authorities as possible. Still, perhaps he'd be able to help out Chester -- In an untraceable capacity? After a few moments -- He takes a deep breath. He then turns his face back towards Chester.

Bobbie: (*resignedly*) All right then – I'll take your word for it. Maybe you're onto something … Let's skedaddle and check out this scene …

It was Bobbie's curiosity and taste for adventure that had made him agree to Chester's proposition. He lets Chester into his car – Chester sits in the passenger seat. Bobbie turns the vehicle around. After driving a short distance, Chester points out a dirt road on the right – Where they turn in. They drive one-quarter mile down the dirt road. Chester tells Bobbie to park the car – Bobbie shuts off the ignition and then they get out. Chester has a flashlight -- Bobbie always carries one as well. They start walking, with Chester leading the way – They veer away to the left of the dirt road and go deeper into the evergreen forest. They walk for another quarter of a mile and then Chester stops Bobbie.

Chester: When I give you a nudge – We'll turn off our flashlights. We'll be approaching the clearing where the ceremony is taking place. The space will be lit up by torches … But first – There's something that I have to tell you. I didn't want to say anything back up at the road, because I was afraid that if I did -- You wouldn't want to come with me to check this place out … I'm a shaman – A shaman for good. Some of the people in this cult are known to me – And I've discovered that they're not for good … And so the two of us will need protection. I'm going to touch your forehead with the palm of my right hand and then you'll be invisible. Now listen carefully -- If for any reason we get separated, you can regain your visibility as follows: You must hug an evergreen tree, close your eyes and then count to one-hundred …

Bobbie *(he repeats those instructions to himself three times)*: Got it.

Chester places the palm of his right hand on Bobbie's forehead -- Bobbie disappears. Then Chester places the palm of his right hand on his own forehead and makes himself vanish … The two of them walk another quarter of a mile. Then, as forewarned – Chester gives Bobbie a nudge. They turn off their flashlights. Twenty-five yards ahead, through the trees, one can see torches and a clearing -- Where people are standing in a circle around a massive pit that has been dug into the ground. Chester and Bobbie make their way towards the clearing and stop ten feet back from its tree-lined edge ... They become aware of two women – They hear the murmur of their conversation. The two females are situated approximately ten feet away, to the left of Chester and Bobbie – They're anticipating the start of the function …

TWO VOYEURS
AWAIT THE MAIN EVENT

Two women wait for the ceremony to begin. They're absorbed in quiet conversation.

Female One: You won't believe how long I've been dreaming about Turmerico Inflammatorio! I know, you're disgusted, and so are all of my other platinum-blonde girlfriends – But he's just so erotic to me! I love the way he mats down that dirty orange combover of his with Vaseline! My platinum-blonde girlfriends are so hypocritical – In the way that they pretend to be repulsed by Turmerico's orange ass hair (hereafter "OAH")! He's famous for his OAH, after all – Or should I say infamous? He literally spun it into gold – Well, at least before he sabotaged the entire enterprise! But I don't care, winner or loser – He'll always be my guru! I know, it's revolting -- You can only talk about the wonder that is *Wonder Fabric Turmerico* with certain people … My platinum-blonde girlfriends are repressed Evilangelists who think human anatomy is gross. To be fair; in some ways it's gross, but in most ways -- It's beautiful! And don't ever let anyone tell you differently! My platinum-blonde girlfriends are behind the times -- Their *conservative family values* did a number on them … By the way, isn't picking up boys in public restrooms a rite of passage for fascist, Isolamickan politicians? I believe those events are referred to as *tea parties* and men who enjoy *tea parties* go to *tearooms*?

Female Two: (*clinically*) You seem to be using an *old school* homosexual slang. And so I must ask you: Do gay, queer or bisexual men still use these euphemistic terms, that are part of a larger homosexual lexicon – That are now looked upon as being dated, derogatory and homophobic?

Female One: I suppose – That could be! (*impatiently*) All I know is that a *tearoom* is a public bathroom that's used for gay cruising! I thought you'd know what that means – It's common knowledge, at least among certain streetwise friends of mine … Now I'm wondering whether I should have brought you here!

Female Two: (*objectively*) I try my best to use expressions corresponding to those that fall under the rubric of the state-of-the-art acronym *LGBTQIA*. By the way: Evilangelists are known for their hatred of LGBTQIA people, who have to keep their wits about them

-- When traveling through the predominately rural areas of a Sub-Region like Heliotrope!

Female One: (*annoyed*) Yes, yes – Of course … Okay, so, you're going by the book; now I see how it's going to be with you -- So let's change things up! (*conspiratorially*) You know what turns me on? A fiscally conservative guy who knows how to break out his ballroom dance moves! He can spin me around, turn me upside down and … Just between you and me, if you can keep a secret that is – He can have his way with me, any way that he wants, every night of the freakin', friggin' week! He can grab me, slap me, spank me! That's right – I'm not above playing games that flirt with violence to heighten the erotic possibilities of a situation … *Heighten and explore!* I'll willingly submit to my ballroom-dancing fiscally conservative guy -- I love to be kinky and rebel against the vestiges of my fundamentalist background in that way! I'll spare you the graphic details – I'll save those for my *rendez-vous* with my man during our *liaison dangereuse*! Because when it comes to sex -- I'm never politically correct!

Female Two: (*impressed*) Wow – You speak French! Do you have a passport? Have you actually traveled outside of Isolamicka! Have you spent time in democratically socialist countries in the Old-World?

Female One: Yes – Yes, I have! … But … Wait a minute … What's going on?

Female Two: I don't know ... I feel strange ... What's happening?

The conscious minds of both Female One and Female Two are responding to an unknown external force. Both of them fall into a trance; it's as if they've been hypnotized -- And their respective personalities have been taken over by spirits ... The two women begin to converse in an ancient and unrecognizable tongue -- In low voices. What Chester hears sounds like Anglo-Saxon – To Bobbie, their speech is incomprehensible ... Then the two women start shape shifting. Female One turns into a ghoul -- Female Two transforms into a gargoyle. After thirty seconds -- They switch identities. After another thirty seconds, Female One and Female Two revert back to their normal selves. Their conversation continues as if they were unaware of what had just happened to them.

Female One: (*sotto voce*) Once I meet my fiscally conservative ballroom dance master, who I'll call Fernando -- I'll become his lobotomized Stepford Wife and we'll enjoy permanent domestic bliss! Picture this: I'll bat my eyes at him invitingly, armed with my weapons of seduction – My platinum blonde hair and my pitch-black irises! I won't have to worry about him giving me what I want, because whatever he wants – I want! I'll even iron his salmon-colored button-down shirts that he wears to his über-corporate, environmentally-raping toxic sludge fund job!

Female Two: (*provocatively*) I have a fetish for seventeenth century Pilgrim clothing, or *couture puritaine*, as you might call it – I wish I could be dressed that way right now!

Female One's jaw drops; after a moment, she starts talking again.

Female One: But more about Turmerico -- I adore his half-hearted attempt at sporting an Eighties New Wave combover! That combover and the extra-long ties of his used car salesman wardrobe are so adorable – They magnify his mediocrity magnificently, I'll tell you that! I mean, Tonie So-Prana was repulsive, but one has to admit – Sister-Woman, that guy was charismatic! The idea of Tonie eating *gabagool* off of my bare ass cheeks and then shoving it into his face – Yeah baby, that turns me on! … He can shove *gabagool* into my face too! I don't care if it's cancerous – I'll take my chances! I WANT IT! I WANT THE GABAGOOL! EVERYONE HAS SOME KIND OF DEATH WISH! AND THAT'S MINE!

But I digress … Here's how I see my life unfolding: I'll marry Fernando Moneda, my fiscally conservative ballroom dance *maestro* and then we'll move into a tacky, nouveau-riche, *So-Pranas*-style McMansion in Joisey! Be it *inferno, purgatorio* or *paradiso*, it will either be Fernando – Or a secret love affair with an Evilangelist sugar daddy! But Fernando's my first choice and here's how it will all go down with him: I'll play the *femme fatale* in a *film noir* and to get what I want, it will involve *le chantage* … That's right: unless Fernando signs a written agreement with me, in the presence of a lawyer, stating that he'll support me financially, for the rest of my life – Then I'll leak information to the press, gleaned from our pillow talk, thereby exposing the jet set liaisons and decadent secrets of this notorious bad boy! … In any case: If all goes as planned, I may very well find the man of my dreams here – Tonight! And then: Let the dominoes fall where they may …

When I look into my crystal ball, this is how I see it all coming together: I'm ensconced in my dream home, my HGTV McMansion in Joisey – Where at long last, I finally have the free time that I've always dreamed of! And when I'm not spending time in my walk-in closet, I'll be chilling in my open concept kitchen – Featuring brick red ceramic floor tile; an olive, indigo and aquamarine backsplash; track lighting fit with soft yellow LED bulbs; a butcher block island with a maple countertop; and a view out of the rectangular-shaped window (behind the deep, stainless steel kitchen sink) of our horticulturally-advanced backyard … At the end of luxurious days that I'll spend imitating sci-fi-B-movie versions of 1950's housewives -- I'll relax and unwind by contemplating nature and communicating with red cardinals! Indigenous cultures believe that cardinals are emissaries of the Great Spirit! Of course, I assume you know that female cardinals are not red – They're pale brown, or brownish-yellow, with tinges of red on their wings … Yes, I'm unhappy about the fact that the Great Spirit unfairly made the female cardinal pale brown. But that will not make me resentful – To the point where I choose to hate the flamboyant plumage of the red male cardinal!

Female Two: (*awestruck*) The way you talk – It's awakening something in me! I feel so confident now! When I hear you speak – It thrills me like an aphrodisiac! How about this: Let's kick off our heels and make a bi-curious adult film together! We can hiss and threaten each other with our venomous fangs -- Like serpents in the Garden of Eden! Let's treat each other like the vicious, sadomasochistic bitches that we truly are! Our film will be called *The Flickering Tongues Of Porn*! What's not to love? Or lust? *Hast du Lust -- Baby?* Just pretend to love me, adult film style – And that will be enough! … We can pretend to be whatever we want to be – We can be 51% male and 49% female, or vice versa! … I'm fine with us using our imaginations – But I do have my limits. For instance: I'm absolutely against the idea of taking hormones! I'm just not convinced that we can truly dispose of the biological sex we were born with -- And successfully transition to whatever sex we want to become …

I guess I'm just nostalgic! I remember the good old days when, besides straight / *cisgender* people – There were mainly *lesbians, gays* and *bisexuals*. According to the Oxford English Dictionary, *transgender* can be defined as: *Those whose sense of personal identity and gender does not correspond with their birth sex.* When I was a child, some transgenders existed -- But they were rare. And occasionally transgenders would transition to the opposite sex via sex reassignment surgery. But is having one's sex surgically reassigned to the opposite sex – The same thing as actually being the opposite sex? ... *Queer* I always understood as being a synonym for *gay*. But perhaps my comprehension of the term is lacking in nuance. According to Wikipedia, queer means this: *not heterosexual* or *not cisgender* ... According to the MedLine Plus Medical Encyclopedia, *intersex* is defined as: *A group of conditions where there is a discrepancy between the external genitals and the internal genitals (the testes and ovaries). The older term for this condition is hermaphroditism.* However these days, if I dared to use hermaphroditism as a synonym for intersex – I'd probably encounter the wrath of a politically-correct mob! Could it be that hordes of staunchly militant LGBTQIAs (or maybe just TQIAs) would storm after me, torches and pitchforks in hand – And threaten me for having used *hermaphroditism* as a synonym for *intersex*?

As for *asexual* – According to Wikipedia, asexuality is: *A lack of sexual attraction to others, or low or absent interest in or desire for sexual activity. It may also be considered a sexual orientation or the lack thereof.* Whereas, for so many years, I thought the term included those who couldn't get laid, or were afraid of sex, or were virgins during high school, or were so lacking in confidence and social skills that they were too terrified to meet anyone – With whom they would have been able to have sex? And of course, at one time or another, I've found myself in all of those situations -- And have experienced insecurity of that nature … That being said, no matter how much life may get me down -- I cannot deny the presence of desire. Are there actually people who do not feel physical sexual urges and that are not overwhelmed, at least in their youth – By their biological sex drives? I'm sorry – But I don't believe it! I just can't believe it! I JUST CAN'T BELIEVE IT THAT ASEXUALITY EXISTS! I CAN'T BELIEVE THAT SEXUALITY CAN BE ABSENT FROM HUMAN BEINGS! I believe that people can be *aromantic* – But not asexual … According to the Oxford Languages Dictionary, aromantic (the adjective) is defined as follows: *having no interest in or desire for romantic relationships.* From that same source, aromantic (the noun) means this: *a person who has no interest in or desire for romantic relationships* … But then, the sexual aromantic (as opposed to the asexual aromantic) refers to a person who, instead of romance -- Maybe prefers a hookup, casual sex, a one-night stand? Or a fuck buddy, friends with benefits, no strings attached? … As for myself, I belong to the category of sexual aromantic, because I do want the sex – I just don't want to be bothered with the romance! Who wants to live with all of that drama and heartbreak? Been there -- Done that! When push comes to shove, what I'm trying to say is this: Aromantic is not an orientation, but rather – A choice one makes in the way that they live their sexual life … And so, without any further *adieu*, here's my proposition: Will you defy gender norms with me? Are you down with that? Are you feeling it? Are you feeling me? WILL YOU DEFY GENDER NORMS WITH ME? YES OR NO?

Female One: (*whispering*) Hey, listen – I'd love to keep discussing this with you … I'm actually happy that you're more open-minded than you first appeared to be – What a surprise! But it looks like the festivities are about to begin! We'll get back to what you were talking about – Let's hush up now … Watch and learn!

The two women become silent and turn their attention to the commencement of the cult ceremony taking place in the clearing.

THE CULT AND ITS RITUALS

The cult members stood at regularly spaced intervals -- Around the edge of the pit. They were dressed in a variety of outfits. One man was disguised as a furry pink Easter bunny, holding a yellow wicker basket full of sky-blue robin's eggs -- In his left hand. Both his human eyes and buck teeth were visible via holes in the face of his rabbit costume – A gleefully sinister expression graced his countenance … *Upon observing the Furry Pink Easter Bunny – A feeling of revulsion welled up from inside Bobbie* … The woman next to the Furry Pink Easter Bunny sported an early-1980s post-punk, art rock look – She wore a sheer black body suit, short black leather skirt with a narrow black leather belt, black leather choker, two black leather bracelets -- And dominatrix-ready, patent-leather black spike heels. All of her leather accessories were embossed with stainless steel spikes. Her short, spiky hair was gelled and dyed blue-black – Her face was covered in clown white makeup. Black eyebrows, black mascara and dark purple lipstick rounded out her look. Her eyes were wide open and the expression on her face was severe. She was fully attuned to the present circumstances …

And then there was the muscle guy with the physique of a high-end porn star. He was sexually charismatic -- His presence and attitude were fierce. He was brawny -- But his muscularity was not extreme, like that of a bodybuilder; he was intimidating, but not a monster. Nonetheless -- His calves and thighs were massive. He wore well broken-in black leather boots that reached up to just below the knee. Each boot included a wide strap, running over the top of the midfoot, that was connected to a brass ring on each side of each boot. He sported titanium earrings, a titanium septum ring and nipple rings -- Black leather bands circled the top edges of his biceps. His large hands, with expertly manicured fingernails – Were covered by black, fingerless leather gloves. He had a thick neck and wore a black latex rubber mask – That left his eyes, nose and mouth exposed. His black leather-belted, black leather shorts covered the top quarter of his thighs – Drawing attention to his considerable endowment; his impressive *basket* was on full display. In the street parlance of classic gay ghetto speak – He could be described as *rough trade* … He was a true bisexual alpha male, the kind that would arouse the interest of women, the desire of gay males and the envy of straight men … Who knows if this mystery fetishist was defined by his look and his lifestyle? It made no difference – Everyone attending the proceedings felt secure within the identity that they were presenting. All of them were there to enjoy the privileges of this secret society -- To which, by all appearances, they belonged …

The rest of the participants, positioned at the edge of the pit, included the following … A businessman sporting a Googo Boss look: black-lensed sunglasses with dark gray frames, a loose-fitting dark gray suit, the quintessential black dress shirt, a tasteful dark gray tie, a black leather belt and sleek black leather shoes -- With slightly rounded, pointed tips … A raven-haired suburban housewife wearing a mid-1960s, sunflower-patterned, sleeveless linen cocktail dress (featuring black, brown and yellow flowers against an off-white background) -- Accompanied by a bright yellow headband and vivid yellow 60's mod-style Mary Janes … A ballerina costumed in a bodice, tutu, tights, pointe shoes and elbow-length evening gloves – All in vivid vermilion … Male and female Wiccans dressed in forest green and earth brown medieval robes -- With hoods and thick rope belts à la *Robin Hood* … Male construction workers attired in royal blue hardhats, indigo coveralls and tan leather work boots … Interspersed around the perimeter of the pit were concrete statues resembling Medusa, Kali Shiva, Hello Kitty, Baphomet and Biff Koontz balloon sculptures ...

And finally, who should be there but Larry and Linda -- The Fun and Lovable Latex Couple, who looked like characters from an updated version of *Gilligan's Island* ... They may have been a little too chubby, in certain elite circles of swingers -- To be taken seriously in their fetish outfits. But they weren't pretending to be porn stars and as much as they were geeky -- They were also supremely confident. They represented an entire world of normal, every-day people – Who just wanted to have fun during their downtime. They didn't care about what any-one thought of them – And that was their gift ... It was unclear, whether Larry and Linda had been granted permission to speak -- At this point in the festivities. Perhaps arrangements for them to do so -- Had been made in advance. They introduced themselves in their strong, Midwestern Sub-Region accents ...

All of the guests that are encircling the pit -- Remain silent and stare straight ahead during Larry and Linda's presentation.

Larry: Good evening, everyone – I'm Larry!

Linda: And I'm Linda! Delighted to be here!

Larry and Linda: (*in unison*) THIS IS A NO-BRAINER, BUT -- WE LOVE LATEX!

Larry: I have a middle-management office job and none of my colleagues have any idea how kinky I am!

Linda: During the holiday season -- I like to make cone-bras for the ladies out of Santa Hats! They always sell out!

Larry: WE are NOT necrophiliacs! That's so not our scene!

Linda: *Eros Thanatos – JOKE!*

Larry: My safe word is *Mirkwood*!

Linda: And mine is *Lantern Waste* …

Larry: And in case this isn't one thousand percent clear already …

Larry and Linda: (*in unison*): We know how to get down with the common people!

Linda: (*opens her arms wide in a welcoming gesture, with a huge and slightly forced smile on her face*) So nice to finally meet all of you!

Larry: We're super psyched to be participating in this event!

Larry and Linda: (*in unison*): See all of you guys later at the orgy!

The floor of the pit, composed of clean light-gray cement – Lay twenty feet down from the top edge of the pit. In the center of the floor, an older man and a middle-aged woman -- Were lying side-by-side on two rectangular-shaped, light-gray cement slabs embedded in the floor. Each slab was seven feet long, four feet wide and three feet high ... The woman was dressed as a scarecrow and the man as a clown. The middle-aged female was wearing a straw wig with a multitude of red-purple bows. She wore purple leather cowboy boots, burgundy painter's pants -- And a viscose-rayon challis fuchsia blouse. Her clothes had been stuffed with hay – Straw was sticking out from inside the waistband of her pants, as well as in-between the buttons of her *chemise*. Copious amounts of ultra-pale blue foundation had been applied to her face. Large vermilion lips, covering the area from just under her nostrils to the bottom of her chin -- Had been painted over her actual mouth. Some charcoal had been randomly brushed across both of her cheeks. A dusty, hippie-style black felt hat sat on the top of her head – It had been added as a final crowning touch ... The older male was dressed in assorted shades ranging from yellow to black. He was sporting an age-inappropriate, bleached blond rockabilly hairstyle – His leather clown shoes were purple. He sported mustard-colored socks with black stripes. The pants of his leisure suit were violet-red and his jacket was magenta. He wore a yellow rayon shirt with a crimson and fuchsia-striped tie. His face was covered with the same ultra-pale blue foundation –As that of his female partner. He wore a fire-engine red clown nose -- Attached to an elastic strap that ran around the back of his head. Large brick red lips, covering the area from just under his nostrils to the bottom of his chin -- Had been painted over his actual mouth.

In spite of the prevalence of bright colors, the overall effect of the couple's clothes and makeup – Was disconcerting. Dark gray circles had been painted over the twosome's eye pairs – Both of their eyebrow pairs had been painted solid black. As the duo lay side by side on their separate cement slabs – They stared straight up, with dead-looking eyes and blank expressions on their faces. The two of them held hands, tentatively – As if they barely had the strength to do so. They looked as if they'd drop each other's hands at any moment … The couple had been drugged – The partners were under the influence of an obscure narcotic. They could see, hear, smell, taste and touch – But they appeared to neither be able to move nor to speak … How had they ended up here? It was as simple as this. The couple had suffered the misfortune of being in the wrong place at the wrong time …

Then unexpectedly, all of those gathered at the circumference of the pit picked up torches that lay on the ground behind them – And lit those firebrands, using torches in front of them that had already been planted at consistent intervals around the top edge of the pit. The participants began to chant:

ORANGE YELLOW FIRE OF LIFE!
BLUE INDIGO WATER OF LIFE!
RED PURPLE BLOOD OF LIFE!
BLACK GRAY WHITE OF DEATH!

They began softly, synchronizing their chanting, gradually getting louder until they reached a fever pitch -- Then they started howling and whooping ... It was then that Bobbie noticed that Chester was now visible (Bobbie himself was still invisible). He continued to observe Chester, who was watching the goings-on intently -- With an odd gleam in his eye ... Bobbie now questioned the motives of this man -- Who'd convinced him to attend this ritual observance, so that Chester could supposedly report the activities of the participating cult members to the local authorities. Bobbie knew how to trust his gut and he thought to himself: *Chester looks like he's really into this ... I bet he's been drawn back into the sect and into whatever degeneracy goes along with that ...* As Bobbie stood in the shadows taking everything in – He struggled to make sense of what he was seeing and wondered how and why a cult like this could have come into existence ... And the conclusion that he came to was this: He'd had enough. He already knew more than he wanted to, about what he'd just witnessed and was sure that any further curiosity on his part – Would only lead to a bad end for him. Secondly, his comrade Chester had apparently been very inspired by what he'd just seen -- And so there was no doubt in Bobbie's mind that Chester had been sucked back into the cult. FUCK THAT GUY -- Bobbie thought to himself … Thus, there was no time to waste: Bobbie stole away, got out his flashlight – And retraced his steps so that he could locate his car. While escaping the proceedings, he suddenly realized that he was still invisible -- He then recalled the words of Chester: *If for any reason we become separated, you can regain your visibility as follows: You must hug an evergreen tree, close your eyes and count to one-hundred* … Aided by his flashlight, Bobbie approached a nearby evergreen, hugged it, closed his eyes -- And then counted to one-hundred. He then pointed the flashlight onto both his left and right hands -- He'd regained his visibility … He soon found his vehicle where he'd left it.

Bobbie had left the party, or more accurately – He'd broken free … But just as he was stepping into his car – He began to hear the cult participants chanting in the distance. Since he'd made his exit – Their chanting of "*Orange Yellow Fire of Life! Blue Indigo Water of Life! Red Purple Blood of Life! Black Gray White of Death!*" had been steadily increasing in volume. Instantaneously -- The sound of that chanting became deafening. Bobbie had to cover his ears

-- As the high-volume chanting was now causing him physical pain.

Then, all of a sudden, an enormous ball of fire exploded in distance – It originated in the area of the pit where the cult ceremony was taking place. It billowed up into a gigantic, moving cloud; Bobbie could feel the heat of the flames and was about to make a break for it -- As he feared the blaze would reach him and burn him alive. But then, just as suddenly as it had appeared, the firestorm vanished in a snap – And was followed by a moment of unearthly silence ... All that could be heard in the aftermath were sounds made by nocturnal creatures of the forest ... Bobbie jumped into his car and hightailed his way out of there. Now he could get back to what he'd originally planned on doing that evening – Before having squandered his time getting involved in who knows what ...

BOBBIE'S DREAMHOUSE

"By the pricking of my thumbs
Something wicked this way comes"
Act IV, Scene I, Macbeth, William Shakespeare

Before having been sidetracked by Chester's invitation to watch the cult ceremony – Bobbie had been on the way to visit his friend Tommie, who lived in a town in the northeastern corner of Heliotrope Sub-Region, Northwestern Region (Neanderthalya), Isolamicka. Bobbie hadn't seen Tommie in ages and he was looking forward to catching up. The two of them hadn't spoken in years, because Bobbie had once said something hurtful to his friend -- That qualified as a *friendship-destroying remark* … However, about one month before the present time, Tommie had called Bobbie, out of the blue -- To tell him that his mother had died. Bobbie was estranged from his own mother and had no interest in finding out -- Whether or not she was still living. In spite of his bitterness – Bobbie could empathize with friends, such as Tommie, who were in mourning. He also hoped that he and Tommie could finally make amends ...

Bobbie drove on; he didn't have far to go now – In five minutes, he'd arrive at Tommie's place. He was shaken by what he'd seen during the cult ceremony with Chester – And was greatly relieved to have narrowly escaped with his life ... The area where Tommie lived was on the floor of a valley. Tommie's abode was a four-story, brick home that had been constructed in 1865. It was situated on the outer edge of a country township – Where neighbors possessed acres of property and maintained a considerable distance away from one another ... Bobbie had seen the place before, in photographs, but upon turning into the driveway of Tommie's home -- Bobbie was in for a shock. The appearance of the house had changed -- So much so that it was now unrecognizable. Although both the front and back of the home (its western and eastern sides, respectively) were shrouded in darkness -- Its northern and southern sides were each lit up, by one floodlight on each side. One floodlight lit up the central section of the northern side of the house – A second floodlight lit up the central area of the southern side of the house. Each floodlight, located halfway between the front and the back of the home – Was embedded in the ground, ten feet away from its respective side of the house ... The effect created by the two floodlights was particularly unsettling -- As the house had been painted black … The front door, its frame, all of the window frames and their shutters, the shingles on the roof and the entire brick exterior – Were completely concealed in satiny, semi-gloss black paint ... All of the house's windows were medium-sized with identical dimensions. There were nine windows each on the northern and southern sides of the house – And six windows each on the eastern and western sides (the back and front sides, respectively) of the house. All of the home's windows were equidistant from one another and there were no windows on the fourth floor … The black house, the floodlights and the preternatural silence gave Bobbie a bad feeling – *How could Tommie live in a house that looks like this?* … With trepidation, Bobbie got out of the car and went to the front door – He was armed and prepared for any potential trouble. He rang the front doorbell, several times – But there was no response … There was an aluminum light fixture above the front door – With a pale, flickering red bulb inside. In the center of the front door, just below the level of Bobbie's chin -- Was a brass knocker featuring the face of a wildcat. Bobbie knocked on the knocker repeatedly; no-one-answered -- Tommie wasn't there … *What had happened to Tommie?* … He then walked to his right, towards the northern side of the house, then along the northern side towards the back side, then along the back towards the southern side, then along the southern side – To return to the front of the house ... As he passed by each side of the home, he looked into the first-floor windows and saw nothing but pitch black. While circling the house, he'd also raised his eyes towards all of the upstairs windows – Not a speck of light was showing through any of those windows ...

Then Bobbie began to feel dizzy -- He sat down on the front doorstep. Gradually, he started to feel like he was high on something – The sensation reminded him of the beginning of a psilocybin trip, when the stomach hurts before the laughter starts ... The tummy ache soon subsided – But then the house and its surroundings began to change. The sky turned from black to gray – And then to a vibrating silver-white with black splotches, like a zebra with a genetic mutation ... Something similar happened to the house – It changed from black, then to gray, and then to white. At first, its color resembled a solid white, but it then morphed into white intermingling with an iridescent silver -- It was as if the house was breathing, as if it was alive. The glare coming from the floodlights turned from white to gray, and then to black, so that *black light* actually shone upon the shimmering silver-white surfaces of the house. Against the luminescent silver-white sky -- The *black light* of the floodlights could now be perceived as light. Bobbie had no idea how he was actually experiencing light that was black – It defied logic. And yet somehow, he was seeing *black light* … In essence, the surrounding area had turned into a high-contrast environment -- *Was this real? Or yet another nightmare?* As he grappled with this altered physical reality -- He determined that he could deal with the fear and that it would not overwhelm him. He would walk through this state of dread because that was what he'd always done – When the going got tough.

He regained his bearings and walked away from the front door, to the right -- To go around the house once again, starting with its northern side … In each of the first-floor windows, as well as those of the second and third floors – There were now figures to be seen, some dark enough to be silhouettes … They were shades from the past who were as pale as death -- Men and women with ghastly, abominable faces. All of them had dark circles around their eyes, two nostril holes underneath an invisible nose and blackened mouths -- Their drawn faces resembled skulls. Some of the specters appeared to be patients in a sanitorium. The eyebrows of the men were thick and unkempt – They looked like derelicts. Their fingers were long and their fingernails resembled claws -- They had warped, gruesome looks and repulsive smiles on their faces. Upon first glance, some had their backs to the windows, until they whirled around with sudden, threatening moves and alarming facial expressions -- As if they purposely wanted to frighten any passersby. These phantoms gave off an air of being trapped -- Like caged big cats or cornered hissing vampires ... There were those that resembled pagans and legendary historical figures as well. One appeared to be Nebuchadnezzar II -- The greatest king of ancient Babylon during the period of the Neo-Babylonian Empire. One looked like Elagabalus -- An eccentric, scandal-plagued Roman emperor. One resembled a nineteenth century, *Wild West,* madam of a brothel – She was busy lighting candles. As she whipped around to face the window -- Her face transformed into that of a sad, wailing shade. One appeared to be an Amourrica Profundan nineteenth century soldier in uniform -- Standing with his head and shoulders slumped over. Blood flowed from his dark eye sockets – A crow was perched on the top of his head, flapping its wings. One looked like a mad scientist -- Complete with a lab coat and wire-frame spectacles. There was a large bald spot on the top of his head -- The rest of his silver-black hair stuck straight out on all sides, like a fright wig. His eyes and nose were jammed together on the top third of his face – A gigantic mouth with crooked, broken teeth comprised the lower two-thirds of his countenance ...

At this point, Bobbie was unable to retreat from the terror and he began to shake. He'd become hypnotized by this spectacle – How could he release himself from its grasp? He summoned his powers of concentration to block all of it out. He stopped look-ing into the windows and hastened back along the southern side of the house – Moving towards the front door, on its western side. Once he'd returned to the front of the house and was sitting on the front doorstep again – The bad trip he'd been on started to recede … Little by little, the sky morphed into light gray, then medium gray and then the black night sky reappeared. The ominously glowing silver-white house reverted to black -- The black house was once again eerily lit by two white floodlights … On that quiet night, with nothing to be heard but crickets -- Bobbie was relieved, yet still unsettled. He now knew for certain that this dwelling that was purportedly Tommie's – Wasn't Tommie's home at all, but rather one that Bobbie had been directed to by a diaboli-cal force ... The apparitions he'd seen in the windows were more than just repressed images from Bobbie's subconscious -- They were real. The specters he'd witnessed were now working in conjunction with the ghosts of his past – That had been crowding their way into his psyche over the years. However -- He would not do the bidding of any of these wraiths. He took some deep breaths and managed to reestablish a tenuous grip on reality … And then, incredibly -- He decided what would have to be done. He hadn't acknowledged it consciously, because he often didn't realize how resourceful he was -- But there'd been a backup plan all along …

Bobbie proceeded as if he were an automaton. He went over to his pine green Chevy Nova and opened the trunk. He fumbled around for the flashlight, found it – And then turned it on. He pulled out a pair of grain cowhide leather work gloves – And put them on. One by one -- He took eight, two-and-one-half gallon containers of gasoline out of the trunk and set them down beside the car … He decided not to break down the front door of the house, as he had a foreboding about the aluminum light fixture above the front door -- With its spooky, flickering, pale red bulb … Instead, he used a hammer that he kept in the trunk of the Nova -- To break the glass of the window nearest to the front door, on the northern side of the house. After breaking the glass -- He used the hammer to knock off the jagged shards protruding from the window frame. He then went back to the Nova and brought all eight of the gas containers over to the now unglazed window, two at a time – And set them down. He then lifted the eight containers through the open window – One at a time. Once those containers had been hoisted through the window – He climbed inside …

Upon entering the home, a half-light came on -- From an unknown source. The wide, centrally-located staircase that ran between the first (ground floor) and fourth floors of the house -- Was bathed in crepuscular light … The house looked bigger on the inside – Than it appeared to be from the outside … Bobbie was greeted by hardwood floors, elegant antique furniture – And black linen curtains covering the windows … He set all eight of the gasoline containers down, two at a time -- By the southern side of the base of the first-floor staircase. He then picked up two of those gas containers – And proceeded up the stairway to the fourth floor. He left the two containers on the fourth-floor landing. He repeated that process – Leaving two containers each, on the third- and then the second-floor landings. He then walked back up to the fourth-floor landing … Something caught his attention when he looked up -- Upon arriving at the fourth-floor landing. He noticed a black wooden ceiling panel, with a black cord and a black, bell-shaped plastic handle on the cord's end -- That led to the *attic* … But the ceiling was too high, rendering the panel out of reach – He was in no mood to linger and he would not investigate that curiosity … He picked up a gas container, unscrewed the cap -- And then set the cap down on the landing. He then walked down the stairs from the fourth-floor landing – Carefully pouring gas, on the right side of the stairway, as he made his way to the third-floor landing. He then used the second container to cover the left side of that same stairway. Those rituals were repeated after he reached the third-floor landing, as well as the second-floor landing -- Four more containers were used in that process. The six empty containers that had been used so far – Were then recovered and left by the southern side of the base of the first-floor staircase. All of the stairs of the staircase, between the fourth and ground floors – Were now covered with gasoline. Only two gas containers remained. The first of those containers was used to cover the ground floor with gasoline -- Starting from the base of the staircase, going through the dining room and then ending at the entrance to the kitchen at the back of the house. The second container was used to cover the first-floor living room – At the front of the home. The final two empty containers were then placed with the others -- By the southern side of the base of the first-floor staircase …

Bobbie climbed back out through the broken window and walked over to the Chevy Nova, to retrieve another item that he kept in the back seat – A box of kitchen matches. Using the flashlight -- He located the matches that were kept in a heavy-duty resealable freezer bag. He opened the bag and then looked inside the box -- There was only one match left … He thought about how in the movies, many house fires were started with just one match -- But now, he wasn't sure if that one match would suffice; after all, he had no real-life experience as a *firestarter*. And come to think of it, had he used enough gasoline – So that the house would actually burn all the way down to the ground? How much had he used? Suddenly he couldn't remember. Inside the house, stood eight empty gas containers -- By the southern side of the base of the first-floor staircase. The evidence was there -- Yet somehow, Bobbie didn't believe that it was real ... He froze; he was stuck – And unable to make a decision. He was furious with himself – For not knowing what to do. The *black house* was ready to be incinerated and he was paralyzed -- How would he resolve this dilemma?

He looked up and noticed a glowing space capsule floating down from the sky. It touched down on the scraggly front yard lawn – A few feet away from the road. After landing, the glowing receded -- Bobbie observed that the ship was made of a silvery, metallic substance. It was an antiquated-looking interstellar vehicle – A relic from the set of *Forbidden Planet*. It was a cone-shaped vessel with a cylindrical top – That resembled an upside-down funnel. The base of the ship had a diameter of fifteen feet – The ship itself was twenty feet high … In the next instant, a being materialized outside of the vessel – She was a human-appearing extraterrestrial who looked like a goddess. Bobbie was mesmerized – The creature had silver skin and a spellbinding presence. She wore an iridescent gold body suit in the style of *Space: 1999*. Her wild and extravagant platinum-blonde hairstyle paid homage to the *Flock of Seagulls*. But she was fearsome as well; radiant white light shone from her eye sockets -- Luminescence also radiated from her open mouth … She stepped away from the interstellar vehicle and moved towards Bobbie. As she advanced -- She put her arms over her head and stretched out her hands. Incandescent light shot out from her fingertips for five seconds – Then stopped abruptly. Bobbie was transfixed … She started to speak -- She enunciated clearly and her voice possessed a soothing quality …

Divine Extraterrestrial Being: My dear, your life has been hard, yet you have persevered – And that is admirable. Now here you are, standing at a crossroads, with your task almost complete – And yet you hesitate. And so I've arrived, like a *deus ex machina* (according to my research, this term has its roots in the extinct language of one of your ancient cultures) … Not to worry – A solution is at hand. Look upon this -- Mortal!

A state-of-the art flamethrower, that Bobbie had once seen advertised on cable TV, appears in her arms.

Divine Extraterrestrial Being: Can you believe your eyes? Do not doubt them – What you're seeing is indeed a state-of-the art flamethrower. As I understand

-- It's legal to own this instrument in your country of Isolamicka. Where did I come across this flamethrower – You ask? Why, I made it myself -- I learned how to materialize 3D objects using creative visualization during my trip to your Blue Green Planet ... Blah blah blah; I won't dally -- I'm here to help you, so that you can move towards your destiny! This weapon can shoot flames up to a distance of 100 feet, about 30.5 meters (I'm so sorry that Isolamicka is still so far behind the times, in its refusal to utilize the metric system). It will be my pleasure to assist you. Now -- I'll go stand by the window whose glass you shattered and I'll do what I have to do …

The Divine Extraterrestrial Being walks over to the broken window, on the front of the northern side of the house – Casually, as if she's on her way to refill a bird feeder. She places herself one meter away from the window -- She assumes a rock star stance and then pulls the trigger. The weapon unleashes a stream of flame that flies through the window -- Reaching the opposite south-facing wall of the house. She shoots flame out from the weapon four more times: To the left, then straight ahead again, then to the right and to the far right as well. The staircase, hardwood floors and black linen curtains -- Start to burn. She then turns around and runs back over to Bobbie, addressing him in great haste:

Divine Extraterrestrial Being: I'll be on my way now – My dear! Your world depletes my strength! May you safely reach your ultimate destination! Whatever fate has in store for you – I wish you all the best and sincerely hope that all of your dreams come true! I must be off! Farewell!

She vanishes. Her silver ship begins to glow and then after five seconds – Rockets upwards into the sky at a fantastic speed. Five seconds after that -- The ship disappears from view and travels beyond the Blue Green Planet's exosphere … The Divine Extraterrestrial Being is now on her way back to the multiverse of her origin …

The fire spread rapidly -- The entire house was soon engulfed in flames and shedding tremendous heat … The expression on Bobbie's face began to change -- His countenance was now contorted and intense. He looked manic, insane -- Berserk … He moved his hands up to the sides of his face, held his fingers tightly together and then extended his arms out in front of him -- With the palms of his hands facing each other. With his fingers still pressed together firmly and with his hands now pointing towards the burning house -- He turned the palms of both hands downwards and then began opening and closing his hands, by shooting out his fingers … *Sorcery was in the air* … The flames were roaring now and Bobbie began to morph into a distortion of his present self. The color of his skin transformed into an iridescent white. His hair turned white – That was streaked with black. His eyebrows, eyes, nostrils, mouth and fingernails turned black … The palms of his hands now faced the house. He kept shooting out his fingers -- As if the palms of his hands were eyes, his fingers were eyelashes and he was making his *hand-eyes* blink …. He was possessed … Whether or not he was conscious of what he was doing -- Bobbie was exorcising the place … The apparitions that he drew out of the home flew into his body and he became their host -- He was fully overtaken and inhabited by phantoms ... Then he started to grow – He grew taller and wider. His feet remained planted on the ground in front of the house – Becoming so huge as to be impervious to the effects of the raging fire. His body stretched out and extended until it had grown to a height of one mile. He kept growing until he reached the upper boundary of the troposphere …

Then who should appear but Pamm Demmyck and Remmy Dessyvyr, who flew by on their broomsticks -- Disguised as *sorceresses à la Bewitched* (Bobbie's upward growth was suspended, as they spoke to him).

Pamm: (*upbeat*) Hey Bobbie! We never talked to you in high school -- Because we didn't know what to make of you. But we thought you were really cute!

Remmy: (*faux-angry*) Yeah – Why didn't you go to more parties? And you never signed my yearbook – You bastard! I cried about that for the entire summer after graduation – And I blame you!

Pamm: She's just kidding ... We only realized years later, as we only had your appearance to go on and knew nothing else about you, at the time – That you were shy, a wallflower. We had no idea what you were going through – As the saying goes: *Everyone is fighting their own battle* ...

Remmy: And you didn't know about our battles either, because you were an introvert, or shell shocked -- Or a victim of post-traumatic stress disorder. And we didn't like the way that you seemed not to care about us, but it wasn't your fault -- Your parents gave you a complex! So it's all good! All is forgiven! That was then and this is now!

Pamm: (*with empathy*) We didn't expect you to reach out to us -- Because we knew that you didn't know how ... For some people -- High school equals the glory days. But for late bloomers like yourself – A glorious post-adolescent future awaits! We support you! We always knew that you were destined to be a shining star!

Remmy: Have a good trip! *Bon voyage!*

Pamm: See you on the other side!

Remmy: BREAK ON THROUGH TO THE OTHER SIDE!

Pamm: ONWARD! BRING IT ON! LET'S ROCK WORLDS!

Pamm and Remmy: (*they simultaneously turn upside down on their broomsticks and then proclaim in unison*) ASCEND TO YOUR GLORIOUS FUTURE – BOBBIE!

Pamm and Remmy laugh gleefully -- As they swerve off and rocket away to their next destination ...

Bobbie's upward trajectory continued -- His feet had now left the ground ... After the troposphere, he continued to rise up through the rest of the successive atmospheric layers of the Blue Green Planet: the stratosphere, mesosphere, thermosphere and exosphere. He broke through the exosphere and entered interplanetary space. By that time, he was so immense that the Blue Green Planet (BGP) was the size of a mere marble -- At the base of his feet. Seeing this opportunity for a moment of supreme power -- He reached down to snatch up the BGP marble and then hurled it, straight ahead of him, with all of his might. He watched the BGP marble rocket away at warp speed and then disappear from view -- It was heading for a void, hundreds of light years away from its Sun, where it would turn into a ball of ice ... Bobbie grew out of the Solar System and traveled through the Via Lactea -- He then left the

Via Lactea and arrived at the edge of the known Universe ... He then moved on to eventual parallel universes and multiverses. He was now big enough to be able to ingest every universe and multiverse that existed. And he did just that -- He consumed everything that existed and became the infinite cosmos. Everything that the limitless cosmos was – Was now inside of him ... He then blew up into a red giant, condensed into a white dwarf – And morphed into a dying sun, set against an endless black void. Then *poof!* ... He was stardust ... All of this was followed by a colossal flash that was The End, *The Opposite of Creation* -- In other words: *The Ultimate Implosion of the Anti-Big Bang*. There ... That was done and now there was Nothing – Nothing except *Nihil, Le Néant* and *Non-Existence* ... *There was Nothing* -- Which does not exist and therefore defies analysis, description and explanation.

"The rest is silence."
Act V, Scene II, Hamlet, William Shakespeare

CODA

And the reason that this unimaginable catastrophe took place was because Bobbie had made the fatal error – Of stopping to pick up Chester, on his way to visit his friend Tommie, on that cool and refreshing autumn night in the northeastern corner of Heliotrope

Sub-Region, Northwestern Region (Neanderthalya), Isolamicka, God-Wanna, Blue Green Planet … Bobbie's fate had been decided -- Once he pulled over to speak to Chester. For it was Chester who'd cast a spell on Bobbie -- At some random point during the cult ceremony, before Bobbie had stolen away to find his car and then escape … It was Chester, who by means of that enchantment had caused Bobbie to grow so large -- That Bobbie was able to consume *Everything That Existed*, during the prelude to *The Ultimate Implosion of the Anti-Big Bang*. By doing so, Foolish Chester had not only sealed his own fate – But that of the infinite cosmos as well.

AUTHOR SELF-PORTRAIT

"Selfie No. Whatever"
Stephen C. Bird, 2021
Smartphone Drawing

ABOUT THE AUTHOR

Stephen C. Bird is a fiction writer and visual artist. Books by Mr. Bird include: "Hideous Exuberance" (2009, 2013); "Catastrophically Consequential" (2012); "Any Resemblance to a Coincidence is Accidental" (2015); and "To Be to Is to Was" (2018). He was born in Toronto and grew up in Erie County, New York. Mr. Bird has lived in New York City for most of his adult life.

"Black Cat. No. 1"
Stephen C. Bird, 2020
Smartphone Drawing

"Types No. 1"
Stephen C. Bird, 2019
Sharpie

"Cat & Building"
Stephen C. Bird, 2021
Collage

"Valentine's Day Card"
Stephen C. Bird, 2019
Collage

"Impromptu Face No. 1"
Stephen C. Bird, 2022
Sharpie & Colored Pencil

"Will The Blue Cat Save Us?"
Stephen C. Bird, 2021
Sharpie

"Sunscape / Landscape"
Stephen C. Bird, 2022
Smartphone Drawing

"Cat & Two Buildings"
Stephen C. Bird, 2021
Collage

'New Face No. 1"
Stephen C. Bird, 2022
Smartphone Drawing